'This is a fantastic, fast p
A very imaginative world c
 mixed with a c
 Ni

'If you like supernatural books and crime novels this will definitely be for you a great mix of the two fast paced and action packed definitely worth a read'
Samantha Wheeler

'I couldn't put it down and read it straight through in one afternoon. Thoroughly enjoyed it and I can't wait for the next Costa and Hoffman book'
Sharron Sayers

'This noir fantasy crime caper brings great characters to life, the heroes will have you rooting for them and the villains are deliciously wicked.'
Gareth Humphreys

H.M.Patel is an avid consumer of storytelling and world creating formats, he reads and writes fictional short stories and holds regular tabletop roleplaying games. From a young age, Computer games and movies captivated his attention, inspiring him to study Video game design and Animation at Teesside University, where he developed a keen sense of story structure and character development.

Noticing the similarities between real-life experiences and his heroes in fictional stories, he embarked on the journey of self-publishing. With the aid of friends and family H.M.Patel writes short crime novellas for Amazon KDP with the hope to one day become a full-time author.

To my brother Gareth,

Thank you

COSTA & HOFFMAN
A MURDER IN AZURITE CITY

H.M. Patel

I

A murder in Azurite City

"Damn! Always at an ungodly hour; why is it always, in the middle of the night you gotta ring me and get me outta bed!?" I always gave Hoffman shit, he gave as good as he got, that was the way we functioned. The other cops sometimes felt it unprofessional, we didn't give a shit. "Always a pleasure to see you too, Costa, I see you still had time to put that junk in your hair" Hoffman replied facetiously.

He loved to complain about my 'poser' attire. Growing up, I watched way too many detective shows and felt I had to dress the part. Long tan pea coat, grey turtleneck and black slacks was my 'go-to look'. Slick Back hair with a sharp undercut was both fashionable and still suitable for the office. Hoffman on the other hand always looked like he was on holiday, bright printed short sleeve shirts, baggy blue jeans and a ruff ponytail holding back greasy unwashed hair. We looked total opposites and behaved like the other looked.

Hoffman walked me down a narrow corridor, flats on either side, this was your typical shit bucket, high rise building. Emerald green walls, black and white chessboard tilling on the floor and dark Mahogany doors with little gold numbering. I hadn't been in this block of flats but it felt like the same block of flats I spend most of my work hours in.

"Victim in her twenties, suffered multiple lacerations across the back and shoulders, hair ripped from her scalp using a rotary tool attached to a rig, and her skin, blistered with multiple layers of calluses, she suffered over a long period of time, this was over weeks, even months, over and over she was tortured, tied up till she healed then

tortured again. This was calculated to every degree."
Detective Hoffman had a way of getting to the point, he'd reel off each gory detail as if he was reading a shopping list, fifteen years of police work in this city will do that to a man.

He wasn't always like this, you don't leave the academy bitter and twisted, but the cold hard truth made him numb, it didn't matter how many cases we'd solve, how many evil psychopaths we'd lock up, how many times we'd follow leads, Azurite City would find a way of delivering more bad news. Everytime we thought we were getting ahead, dead end, after dead end. Crime had a way of covering itself up in this city. There'd always be another freak around the corner worse than the previous one. Honestly, it took a toll on us both. Was it healthy? No, but nobody was willing to do the dirty work, or at least try. That's what I admired about Hoffman, he'd follow me to the end, there wasn't any line he wouldn't cross, no red tape would stop him. No order from the chief that would deter him from catching the scumbag responsible. Were we boy scouts? No, we did, what we had to do, and we got the job done.

Hoffman opened the door; the room lacked any furniture, no TV, no couch, hell, no kitchen, just an empty shell. The perp had rented the property specifically to torture and murder victims. In the centre of the room was a pool of blood with a wooden chair, the victim naked, her ankles zip strapped to the chair legs, the rig Hoffman had mentioned behind her, towering over her like a spider, eight arms encapsulating her like a split cocoon.

"Take a look here" Hoffman pulled a pen from his jacket pocket and lifted the victim's hand from the chair's armrest.

"Have you seen anything like this before?" On the palm of her hand was a symbol, raw and blistered like burnt caramel. I took my phone out to take a picture and the symbol moved, revolving in a violent motion till it peeled itself off the victim's skin and vanished. I looked at Hoffman, he had the same look in his eye, I could tell he was thinking the same as me; Worlocks!

At two in the morning, it wasn't worth starting a full day of investigation so we decided to call it there, a fresh day, a fresh start. Hoffman could see I wasn't in the best of moods to start bashing doors down, especially if we were right, Worlocks aren't to be messed with. I made my way back to my apartment; two blocks south, after being in that room I needed the fresh air plus ten bucks for two blocks was the going rate in this city, I didn't have that kinda free cash, so I walked, planning the next day in my head, probably muttering odd words out loud, must have looked as mad as one of those freak shows at st.Abigail's home for the insane. I reached my tower block and looked at my watch, 'six hours left, not bad, get a good night's sleep in that.' I could hear Nyx clawing at the front door. Nyx, my panther, department issue guardian. The day after graduating from the academy, Hoffman received an owl and I got a panther, I never let him forget that. How on earth is an owl gonna save you in this city? Nyx was a docile creature, loved sleeping in the corner of my living room, never bothered for anything, that is unless I was in danger, she'd turn into a real beast to protect me, always did her job, I loved that girl. I opened my front door and shewed Nyx away with my foot. She looked at me with those bright blue dopey eyes, I could never understand cruelty to animals, they have a way of knowing exactly what you're thinking, staring into Nyx's eyes was like gazing into a deep ocean, intense, rich blues swirling majestically. She paused, looked at my arm and bit me, took a chunk clean off, Nyx had never shown aggression to me at all, what? Why? Blood poured everywhere; she knew I had healing powers so I wasn't in any danger, but still, God damn that hurt. I grabbed a towel to mop up the blood, and whispered a healing spell.

"Nirowheem-halindarl, shlaargh-envhool, drol-deghaal"
my arm healed, but the extent of the bite left a hefty scar, didn't bother me but It did mean I would have to report this to HQ, probably meant Nyx getting re-assigned, And that did bother me.

In the morning I harnessed Nyx and headed off to the precinct. Nyx didn't need a harness, but I wasn't taking any chances. she looked real sorry for herself and sluggishly wondered behind me, was I doing the right thing? Why the hell did she bite me? I had to follow protocol on this one, a misbehaved guardian is a real problem, who knows what kind of issues she might have in the field. I clocked in and took Nyx to the precinct vets; Dr Harlow knew everything about guardians, surely if there was anything we could do for Nyx, she'd know.
"Doc, we got a problem!" Dr Harlow turned around, short black hair tied up in a ponytail, creamy lavender skin and an hourglass figure. A Noxsierian goddess, she was both brilliant and beautiful, she spoke in a thick, old fashioned

English accent, such class and elegance. Noxsieria was a planet off the Yamda galaxy, due to an unstable atmosphere the air became toxic and was uninhabitable, most of the Noxsieria moved to earth centuries ago. The Doc and I had an unofficial relationship a while back which turned into the odd meaningless sex now and again, nobody knew about it, we kept things professional. I always wondered why she worked at a rundown, underfunded little precinct with commoners like me and Hoffman, but she never let on, never looked down on any of us.

"Doc, it's Nyx" I showed her my scar. "I came home from a crime scene and she was clawing at my front door, then with no warning, she took a pretty big chunk out my arm" Dr Harlow looked stunned

"You've been with Nyx for quite some time now, how long?" she looked through the records on her computer "Wow! Twelve years, and you've had no previous issues with her" she walked over to Nyx to check her vitals, "she doesn't seem off, best leave her with me for a couple of days, I'll run some tests and I'll keep you posted" I handed the lead over to the Doc "please, whenever something comes up, let me know" Doc smiled sympathetically "will do"

Hoffman left a stack of evidence on my desk; I began to flick through his notes when I felt a searing pain in my head, my jaw began to stiffen, the background noise of the precinct became tinny and muffled, it felt like I was under water. I fumbled into the second draw of my desk for some painkillers, two left. As I crunched them down

the pain got worse, my jaw seized totally shut, I reached for my phone and messaged Hoffman "Somethings wrong, meet me at my place!" I rushed home, stumbling around like a drunkard, each step trying to catch myself, desperately trying to keep it together. I managed to get home. My skin started to tingle, it felt like ants crawling all over my body, something was wrong. I jumped into the shower and ran the water cold, I could feel my skin turning numb. The water was so cold I couldn't catch my breath, desperately trying to cool off and calm these symptoms, what was going on? Did I catch a bug? I'd never felt like this. Hoffman came running in
"I got your message, what the hell!?" he barged in my bathroom and found me propped up against my bathtub naked, the symptoms started to fade at this point. I mumbled
"Nyx bit me! Call the Doc" Hoffman grabbed my phone. "Costa! You've got three missed calls from the Doc!" Hoffman handed me my phone, "two messages as well?"

"Detective Costa, call me back it's urgent, Nyx's vitals are through the roof"

"I'm sorry, Nyx didn't make it, please come in, I have some details we need to go over"

I put my phone down and looked at Hoffman, "It's Nyx, she; she didn't make it" Confused, Hoffman replied "Didn't make it? you got bit? How'd she die?" I steadied myself and got changed

"We gotta find out, Doc's got the details. You good to drive?" Hoffman handed me my shirt and grabbed my badge "c'mon, let's go" Hoffman parked the car just outside my apartment block, the drive was only a couple of minutes but felt like hours. Nyx was in perfect health, how did we both get sick at the same time? I mumbled questions over and over in the car, none of this made any sense. I got to Doc's office as fast as I could, "Doc! Where's Nyx?" Doc tilted her head from her computer screen "Detective Costa! Come with we" she began questioning my previous cases "Detective; are you on a particular case personal to you?" puzzled, I looked at her and shook my head

"no, me and Hoffman just attended a murder scene early in the morning, there wasn't any connection to either of us?" I stopped her

"Do you think someone attacked Nyx?" Hoffman interjected "someone may have attacked you both! Doc! Costa just had life threatening symptoms of his own, locked jaw, cold sweats. He didn't look too good!" Harlow sharply turned to Costa, "Both of you? With the same symptoms? I've never seen a connection between a detective and guardian like that" we entered Doc's lab, sterile and meticulous. I didn't expect anything less. In front, laid Nyx on a steel table, her skin was blistered and calloused like the victim from the previous night's crime scene. The same symbol burnt on her neck. I held her in grief "Detective Costa, could you describe the symptoms you felt?" I stood up straight, removing my arms from Nyx's torso "uh, Severe head pain, locked jaw and tingling skin." Doc looked at her notes on her clipboard, she started to smile sympathetically.

"Detectives, reading through the notes here, the crime scene you both went to had a Worlocks curse, this curse latched onto Detective Costa and began to set its poison, it's because of Nyx you're alive" Doc Harlow walked over to me and placed her hand on my shoulder

"Nyx, did her job, she bit your arm and transferred the curse to herself. You suffered some of the poison, which explains the way you felt earlier, but Nyx suffered the same poison in a much higher dose, she didn't bite out of aggression, she bit you to protect you"

"Damn" Hoffman muttered under his breath.

"These guardians never cease to amaze me, trained to protect their handlers at all costs, they have senses we could never imagine" I looked at Hoffman with anger and wrath in my eyes

"We need to pay a visit to Pavlov at the Arcane Abyss."

II

Twenty years earlier

Crime in Azurite City was at an all-time high, Police funds were stretched so thin, there were complete districts unmanned and unsafe, the local militia and rebels had taken over and declared themselves the law, they felt policing should be enforced by their own. People weren't afraid of breaking the law, In-fact lawbreaking became a way of survival. Detectives Costa and Hoffman were in their first year of the academy, blind hopefuls ready to take on crime and change the city for the best. At this point they didn't really know each other, the class of '05 consisted of eighty five pupils, the initiative to boost police numbers was given the go ahead by the city mayor Alyssa Reed. Ms Reed wasn't like any other mayor Azurite city had the pleasure of having, she cared about the people, wanted the best for its citizens and was ready to do what was necessary, she was exactly what this city needed. Ms Reed's first mission, increase police presence and stamp down on the gangs plaguing the streets.

Azurite city had three main factions, the Electric Dragonflies, Dark Watch, and the Crimson Guard. The Crimson Guard were the largest of the three but individually the weakest. They were only known for their thuggish behaviour. They didn't even own any real weaponry and would mostly use fists when fighting. Their members were all high schoolers or younger, which made sense because that's how most gang members seemed to start out at first. They came from poor families and their parents were too worried about their children going astray. It was unfortunate that they ended up being forced into such dangerous work and couldn't get away from it.

The Crimson Guard was led by an older man named Willem. He had been with the group since he was young, he even managed to defeat a member of the Electric Dragonflies, making him quite famous. There were many rumours swirling around about what happened behind the scenes, though. Some said that it wasn't a fair fight; others claimed that Willem attacked the Electric Dragonflies while they were at war. Whatever the case may have been, the more people who knew about it, the more renown Willem got, sometimes, in this case renown is not always a good thing. Willem was murdered in his sleep, it was said to be an act of retaliation, acted out by someone from the Electric Dragonflies. Nobody knows for sure.

In contrast, the Electric Dragonflies were the best Worlocks in Azurite City. They had good equipment, trained every day, and had a lot of respect among the wizards of the city. Their leader, Sir Nikita Pavlov, was an arrogant bastard who liked to show off his rank and his abilities, he enjoyed playing practical jokes on innocent people, most of the time leading to death or dismemberment. Pavlov had a cruel nature, picking on the weak and defenceless, Pavlov made deals with politicians and landlords to raise taxes sky high for the citizens of Azurite City, of course Pavlov took a cut. The Dragonflies were tolerable but Pavlov was to be feared.

The Dark Watch were regimented Fascists, the men had been conditioned to abide by the orders of their superiors and never stray. Sgt. Abara moved with a peculiar

grace—not quite an athletic stride but something closer to a dance or a martial movement. He walked alone, his back straight, head high. The soldiers followed him without question, admiring his every move.
They passed the central fountain everyday where children splashed and played in the spray. One day oblivious to the tension around them. A young woman stood on a balcony above the square, watching her child play. She wore a pale blue dress and waved happily when she saw them coming. Her arms were full of flowers and she held them out to one of the officers. with a swift backhand, he batted them out of the way, nearly sending her sprawling onto the ground. Abara had noticed this behaviour and came to her aid, "Apologies, are you ok?" stunned in his aura, she giggled and looked away. Abara gently held her chin and pulled her gaze toward him, "Such Beauty, Please" gesturing to her to stand. As she did, his demeanour turned sour. Darkening the skies around him he grew in stature, his eyes glowed red. In silence he left and joined the march, his face stern and cold. That was the typical behaviour of the Dark Watch, it did not sit well with most. The mother dropped all of her flowers and ran back into her apartment.

The three factions were at war; The Great War, as it would become known, lasted for seven years and resulted in the deaths of some five million people, mostly from disease or starvation. All three gangs suffered heavy losses. But when the smoke cleared and the fighting fell silent, one side clearly emerged victorious. The Dark Watch. It wasn't a surprise really. battling a group of local thugs and a band of rich, witless fools, it was obvious the Dark Watch could not be stopped by any force on Earth.

As soon as the smoke cleared and the dust settled, the leaders of the Dark Watch turned their attention to another threat: the growing power of the Police force. While they had been able to dominate the streets after the Great War, there was still plenty of resistance. Some areas remained stubbornly free of the Dark Watch's iron grip. The police responded by building up their own forces and forming alliances with other law enforcement agencies throughout the world. Slowly but surely, the Dark Watch went from a fascist regime to a few small loyal individuals staying true to the Dark Watch ways, hiding in the shadows while the rest of the world grew prosperous once again.

Officers Costa and Hoffman were key to this turn in Azurite City, the determination to make the place safer and clear the gang's tyranny rendered themselves heroes in the precinct. They knew how dangerous it was to get into a fight, but they couldn't just sit around and wait for someone else to do something about it. There would be hell to pay for if anyone underestimated the lengths these two officers would go to. So far, their efforts had paid off well; though their initial attempts at cracking down on the gangs had ended up with them in far too many close calls, that didn't stop them from trying again. With their relentless efforts they gained rank, a promotion to detective. Now, considered amongst the most skilled detectives in the city. It wasn't long before they became a force to be reckoned with, able to take down any criminal who dared threaten the safety of the city

By the time the next election came around, only one person stood out as a real contender for President, Alyssa Reed. Alyssa had proven herself as mayor and greatly improved the lives of her people. She grew up in a rough neighbourhood and could physically look after herself, this made her tough and resilient, but she had a soft heart that won the people's trust. After resolving the great war and restoring peace in Azurite City, the locals came to love her. As president, she continued her work by helping those in need. Alyssa worked very closely with Costa and Hoffman, pulling strings under the table enabling the two detectives to get the job done when others couldn't. The three of them were a perfect team.

III

The disappearance of Officer Abara

After the War Sgt. Abara left the Dark Watch and joined the Police force. Leaving a fascist regime to then lead a police force was a pretty tough U-turn, He was hated by many of his peers, both criminals and officers, but that did not affect him in any way. He had a job to do regardless of which uniform he wore.

Somehow he always seemed to be in the right place at the wrong time. His first day on the job he shot a man who had broken into a school. The man was mentally unstable and believed he was a student attending classes, unfortunately, a local cop had seen the whole thing and gave evidence against Abara. Abara spent a year locked up in St. Abigails. When they found no evidence that his actions were unjustified the case was closed and he was released back onto the streets, with a full pardon.
The following five years saw Abara rise through the ranks and become one of the most decorated officers in the police force. However even after all those medals he still wasn't liked by everyone. Some people thought he should have been executed for what he did on his first day of work. Others felt that he took justice too far and brought back old traditions that were abolished long ago.
After some hard work, he became a symbol of righteousness and justice. A man who would go above and beyond to protect those from anyone who threatened them. They watched as he led raids against drug dealers, rapists, murderers and any other criminal that dared cross the line. All while being a single father to his son.
No matter how much criticism he received, he continued on fighting for what he believed in. After all, he had sworn

an oath to serve and protect the citizens of Azurite City and that's exactly what he intended to do.

"I can't believe it... With each promotion my life gets more crazy." Sgt. Abara muttered words under his breath to himself. His entire career had been dedicated to fighting crime, making sure things got better for everyone. After all, going back to a fractured city was the nightmare he had feared, the screams of innocent children haunted his dreams, defenceless civilians at the mercy of violence. Sitting down on the couch he picked up a photo that sat on the table next to him. In the picture Abara was holding his newborn son in his arms. "This is what matters." He said looking at the smiling face of his son. He sat alone in his apartment staring at the walls trying to figure out where to start. It was early morning and he had just returned from a raid on a gang operating in the slums outside of town. Abara's phone rang
"I wonder what the boss wants this time..." He said to himself, Looking at the caller ID - 'Samira'
A woman spoke softly to him "Sergeant Abara? This is Samira. We've received word from our contacts that you're needed at the Precinct right away." She said,

"What's going on?" Asked Abara

"We just intercepted a message from an agent at the Golden dragon." Answered Samira. "They want to meet with you."

"Alright tell them I'll be there in an hour!" He said hanging up the phone.

After a short drive Sgt. Abara arrived at the city's main police station. A dilapidated building with old stone doors and gargoyles facing the front porch. The sergeant got out of his car and walked towards the front entrance which opened automatically as he approached. He advanced cautiously inside, something wasn't quite right. The front desk was empty, the usual manic chaos was instead an ear piercing silence. He stopped dead in his tracks and looked around the lobby as if expecting to see someone. Abara turned to face the entrance, as he did he was faced with a hulking figure. The figure grunted and whacked Abara over the head knocking him unconscious. Abara, dazed and confused, was dragged by his shoulders into a dark room and slammed against the wall hard enough to knock the wind out of him. His eyes barely open he could make out a shadowy figure in the corner of the room.

"You really think you can wipe away the past and wear that uniform!?" A voice demanded answers from the shadows.

"Who are you!?" Abara asked, rubbing his sore ribs.

"After all these years, you've forgotten me, I'm insulted!" The ominous voice from the darkness shouted. Then softy sighed

Abara stared into the corner of the room, looking for anything that could help him identify the person speaking to him, his face pressed into the tiled wall with his arm locked behind him. The Giant from the police foyer pushed into Abara's body, rendering him useless.

"Who are you!? What do you want!?" Abara demanded answers,

"Ah," the figure chuckled to himself.

"Me first! Do I look like; a monster to you?"

Abara stood there for a moment, thinking carefully before answering.

"I can't see your face! Show yourself!"

"Yes, this is what you did to me!" The figure advanced slowly, dramatically revealing his face into the light.

A smartly dressed man in a black pinstripe suit, slick black hair and mirror finish black oxford shoes - the soft scent of vanilla and tobacco aftershave filled Abara's senses.

"If I remember correctly the last time we met, you shot me in the forehead with an enchanted rifle." He said pointing at the hole in his head. "You even broke my jaw."

Horror struck Abara as he remembered the Great War

"Pavlov!" He exclaimed with a slight questioning tone.

"So, you DO remember me then!" Pavlov screamed in excitement.

"How did you survive!?" Abara asked.

"There are things in this world that your kind never understood." Pavlov answered. "Things that you don't need to understand."

Abara just stood there dumbfounded not knowing how to respond.

"Don't worry about it though, I've come to offer you a deal. I know everything you did. I also know what happened to the Dark Watch." Pavlov leant in close to Abara's face whispering in a sinister tone "I know your secret."

Abara wasn't sure what to say or do, he knew Pavlov uncovered secrets about the Great war, secrets only the leaders of the old gangs knew, secrets that could ruin everything Abara had worked for.

"Let me go and we won't have any issues." He said. "I am an Officer of the law, you cannot do this. Times have changed Pavlov!"

"Oh I wouldn't dream of just letting you go! That would ruin my plans"

Abara stood there shaking, his mind racing as he tried to comprehend what was happening.

"So you see," Pavlov continued, "We are the only ones left from the Great war and I'm not going anywhere. So what's it gonna be? Do you wanna fight or do you want to join me?"

Abara just stood there, struggling to make sense of the situation.

"Well? How about it?"

Abara clenched his fist with anger and ground his teeth "Why would I join a lunatic like you?"

"Stop being a fool!" Pavlov shouted. "Or do you want me to kill ALL of the people you love?

Abara was stunned, his eyes darted back and forth as he questioned who he might be talking about

"awww, poor Sathia, or Samira, or Samantha…meh same thing, right?" Pavlov chuckled to himself "you haven't even asked about your lovely paramore?"

Abara's eyes began to widen as he realised who called him to the precinct.

"Samira!" He screamed.

"what have you done!" He demanded answers.

Pavlov laughed as he pulled out a polaroid

"She looks very different these days, did she do something to her hair?"

Abara looked at the picture in horror. Samira slumped naked, tied to a chair with a metallic spider-like contraption towering behind her, eyes sewn shut. The man in the picture held a glowing knife, holding it to her wrist.

"I can hear her screams from inside this very building." Pavlov said as he pointed at the room's ceiling.

As Abara glared at the picture, he felt sick to his stomach.

Pavlov laughed as if he knew something that Abara didn't. Pavlov could feel the rage radiate off Abara's body.

"What have you done to Samira!" He screamed, failing to struggle free "where is she!"

Pavlov laughed again

"Me? That is not me in the photo, I haven't done anything!" Pavlov shrugged off the accusation, whilst picking the dirt from his nails

"Join me Abara" Pavlov sat backwards on a chair and zoomed in close to the sergeant, almost touching noses "Join me and save your Boss!....your lover!" Pavlov pleaded

Abara's eyes glowed red, this made Pavlov laugh even harder.

"You don't understand! I don't want to hurt the girl, well…anymore. You're making me do it" he said with a sarcastic smile.

Abara sighed and whispered "What do you want?"

Pavlov could see the defeat in his eyes, he then reached into his pocket and pulled out a small clear orb. He held it up so Abara could see.

"This will teleport us back in time to before the Great War!" Pavlov said as he gazed into the orb.

Pavlov darted his gaze at his henchman, and nodded towards the door, signalling him to leave, the giant pulled back from Abara and left the two alone in the room.

Pavlov smiled as he spun his chair around, folding his arms and kicking his legs on the desk, making himself comfortable. Pavlov was in total control and loved every second of it.

"Wouldn't you like to save your fellow soldiers?" He asked "to know exactly what's going to happen, just before it does and defeat your enemies with ease."

Abara gazed into the orb, temptation took over him. He then remembered Samira.

"What about Samira?" Abara exclaimed through gritted teeth

Pavlov looked at Abara and smiled

"She will join our cause, she will make sure the police of Azurite city won't bother us on our.....quest"

Pavlov held the orb at arms length and pointed it to Abara "Shall we?" He asked

Abara looked at the orb and nodded his head reluctantly. As they both touched the orb a vortex of crackling purple energy engulfed them. Pavlov watched as Abara disappeared from sight. Pavlov had tricked Abara, sending him to another dimension, allowing Pavlov to wreak havoc with nobody to stop him. Pavlov turned and walked away leaving his henchmen to guard the building. "Kill the girl!"

"Too easy" Pavlov laughed under his breath, tossing the orb repeatedly into the air feeling pleased with himself. Descending down the police stations entrance steps, passing the gargoyles above he waved his hand and transformed the precinct from an old stone building, to a gothic nightclub, a dark mahogany structure with stained glass windows which kept the light from entering the building. he looked at the sign above the door reading 'ACPD' scoffing under his breath he waved his hand one last time 'Arcane Abyss' "Better!"

# IV

Investigation at the Arcane Abyss

Hoffman and I arrived at the club's carpark, The Arcane Abyss was a local spot for the magical community, Worlocks, Wizards and Sorcerers were regularly seen at all times of the day. The club was notorious for drug dealings and trafficking, but untouchable because it was under Pavlov's protection. We arrived at the club's front door and were greeted by a former policeman working as a bouncer. He was in Arcane Abyss uniform, A red skin tight t-shirt, black baggy camouflage trousers and tan combat boots laced tight to his shins, He had a utility belt on with several weapons clipped in, a fully loaded handgun holstered under his arm.

"How can I help you boys?" the bouncer said with a deep gruff, looking over our shoulders to the queue forming behind. "Clearly not here for pleasure!"

"We're looking for Pavlov," Hoffman replied "Need to speak with him?"

"He's in the back. I'll need your weapons before I can let you pass, just protocol lads."

Hoffman rolled his eyes. "Are you serious?" Hoffman flashed his badge

"Don't care" the bouncer clearly got angrier as he could see the queue getting longer "Nobody gets in with weapons!" Hoffman glanced at me and shook his head as he handed his revolver over to the bouncer. I unclipped my pistols and placed them in the tray next to the bouncer. "Not exactly standard issue" the bouncer looked at them in shock. Two black desert eagles modified with reflex sights and carvings on the handles, one with Lucifer holding a chalice, the other with the archangel Gabriel wielding a longsword.

The bouncer replied in a calm manner "If it makes you feel better I'm not going to ask why you want to see him so badly." The bouncer really got on my nerves, the fucking cheek. I hate incapable coppers ditching the force and working for the enemy, this happened way too often. The department spent the taxpayers money training these goons up, just so they could abandon the people and swap sides, disgusting.

"Good! It's none of your business anyway!" I swiftly replied denying any authority the bouncer may have thought he had

The bouncer looked us both up and down before putting our weapons in the locker to the right of him. He unlocked the heavy steel door and motioned for us to enter. Loud rock music filled the room, drowning out the sound of people talking. The room was dimly lit, giving the place a creepy vibe. Dark red strobe lights and a thick fog, Hoffman and I walked slowly through the club, keeping an eye out for anyone unsavoury who might have recognised us.

The large bar ran along the east side wall, there were several empty tables scattered about the room. A few members of the magical community were socialising, taking no notice of us. Good. The bartender, A small slender elf wearing a red cocktail dress served drinks to the punters. Hoffman and I walked towards the bar where a young woman stood. I leaned over to the bartender, "We need to speak to Pavlov!" flashing my badge, with arrogance, like she'd be impressed somehow. The Bartender shook her head in disgust and carried on wiping a glass, she pointed to the glass office on the second floor with her elbow. I could tell we were not welcome and to be fair, I wanted the hell out of there. I felt on edge, at any moment things would kick off and the odds were not stacked in our favour.

We climbed a flight of stairs and entered a large office, a delicate wooden desk sat in the centre of an empty room, four glass walls and a bright red carpet matching the decor of the nightclub. An ornate sculpture of a werewolf stood central facing the entrance. The chair behind the desk swivelled to face us.

Pavlov was an older man, bald with a long tailored beard, he appeared to be in his late sixties. His grey eyes piercing even in this dull light, his skin pale wrinkled from years of battle. I felt an unease around him, I knew that he was one of the most powerful mages in the city. He was also a notorious killer, known for his black magic spells and dark rituals. The man was a walking textbook of evil.

"What can I do for you today?" Pavlov asked, he spoke with a deep voice and a slight accent, it sounded more like a Scottish or Irish brogue than anything else.

Hoffman took a step forward, as he did he noticed a dog sitting next to Pavlov, they locked eyes for a moment "This is my Partner Detective Costa, I'm Detective Hoffman"

Pavlov nodded and held his hand up "Please!...I know who you are" he paused for dramatic effect and then continued. "You're the two detectives who put a stop to the terrorist attacks last month. I heard rumours that it was you who got those terrorists off the streets..Bravo!" Pavlov slowly clapped his hands patronisingly

Hoffman coughed awkwardly trying to think of something clever to say.

"So what brings you here today? I'm assuming it's not small talk you're after."

Hoffman remained silent and slightly tilted towards me

Walking towards Pavlov I explained "We're investigating a murder" as I got close, I slammed a handful of polaroids on his desk, each showing a harrowing image of the tortured victim and the bloodied crime scene.

"These were taken yesterday, the poor girl suffered for a long time. Some sick twisted bastard did this, and you know who!" I loved to press hard when questioning suspects, asking the right question worded just right, made most people flinch. Pavlov unfortunately didn't, this meant he either knew we needed more evidence or knew he'd get away with it regardless. The images didn't affect him in the slightest, that told me more about his character than the crime, he'd seen violence like this before.

Pavlov chuckled "Oh really? What proof do you have?"

Signs of torture, the spider-like contraption and the Worlock's signature scar on her wrist. you gonna tell me you had nothing to do with this?"

Pavlov waved his hand dismissing my evidence. "This looks like the work of anyone in the magical community, I have no idea who this person is, but I doubt they would associate with me."

"Listen you old bastard! I know all about you and your dark dealings. I've been investigating you since I joined the force. I know how much of an influence you have over others and how you use your power to control people."

Pavlov leaned back in his chair smugly, "I'm afraid I don't know what you're talking about." He laughed again as if he was enjoying some great joke.

"Stop playing your games!" Hoffman shouted!

He stood up from behind his desk, "Fellas, if you have any real evidence, please call. I'd be happy to come down to your precinct and help any way I can. Otherwise, don't waste my time, I am very busy!" He gestured to us to leave his office. "Please, help yourself to a drink, on me" he smiled in an ironic *'we both know i'm guilty'* sort of way.

Hoffman and I left Pavlov's office and headed over towards the bar, the bartender looked up when walked past her. "Can I get you anything?" Hoffman thought about it for a second, I could clearly see the case was getting frustrating for him and the temptation of drowning the day away was a viable option at this point so I answered before he could get a word in. "Sorry, on duty". We left the club collecting our weapons. "So, where now?" Hoffman had a bewildered look on his face with a slight hint of anger, I knew he wanted to just barge back in, slaughter the lot of them and obliterate the existence of that corrupt, twisted evil man; Hell, so did I, but we had to do things by the book, if we followed procedure we'd do things the right way. "He'll have friends to vouch for any alibi he cooks up, we need hard evidence" I said. "Let's go back to the crime scene, see if we can get a lead"

Local PD made an attempt to protect the crime scene, but with a crowd of journalists and rubberneckers milling around, anybody could have entered the apartment at this point. I pulled up just in front of the building "Fuck sake!" looking at the mass of hysteria gathering around the building "Can we clear the area please!" I flagged two cops "You! Push back the crowds to make sure they don't get close to the entrances, we still have residents in the building, they'll need access" I looked at Hoffman and shook my head, Hoffman grinned "wouldn't have happened in our day ay?"

The cops nodded and cleared the area around the crime scene. I stood outside the door and shouted over to a male officer in front of the entrance "What happened here?" looking at a pool of blood coagulating on the floor he replied "A fight, some weird bastard broke in, left the kid like this, beat the hell out of him!" Hoffman rushed up to me and demanded answers, "Do we know who did this?" the officer replied "I heard from the residents, they heard shouting, then a man stormed in, ran right into him, knocked him out cold and shoved him here" he pointed towards the body. "What about the other residents? They seen the man?" I asked "they didn't hear anything. Just heard the fighting" Hoffman pulled out his revolver and gave me a nod signalling me to cover him as he entered the building. I followed suit, stepping in with my pistols raised, both ready for anything. The corridor was dark, the lights had been smashed in the struggle. Blood smeared the walls and the carpet, we stepped carefully, trying not to disturb any evidence. We made our way up the stairs towards the apartment. I put my finger to my lips, signalling for Hoffman to stay quiet. He nodded his head in agreement. Hoffman and I perfected this technique back in our early days as beat cops in uniform, this was routine for us. We continued slowly up the stairs, turning the corner and headed towards the door. As we entered the crime scene, we found it ransacked, evidence was strewn all over the room. I signalled to Hoffman and pointed to the bedroom, he nodded and headed there first.

Hoffman entered the room first, I covered right behind him, aiming over his left shoulder. My aim darted at the window as a shadowy figure rushed past. "Over there" I shouted, Hoffman followed me as we chased the mysterious figure, I watched as the figure turned a corner at the end of the hallway. As I rounded the corner, I saw a figure climbing through the window at the end of the hall. "He's climbing out!" I shouted. I drew my pistol and aimed at the figure, "don't shoot" Hoffman grabbed me by the wrist, stopping me from firing. "We need him alive!"

The figure climbed through the window and fell into the alleyway below, the sound of a body hitting the floor was clearly audible. Hoffman and I rushed out the window, we ran across the roof of the building and followed the alley down towards the street. The figure had already disappeared from sight, we heard footsteps heading around the corner, so Hoffman and I made chase. We rushed around the corner just in time to see the figure jumping into a car. I opened fire, the windshield shattered as the bullets penetrated the car's exterior. The car peeled off with screeching tyres, spinning as the figure changed gear. "Fuck!" In frustration I kicked a trash can over Hoffman holstered his revolver and rested his hands on his hips and leaned back. "Now what?"

Hoffman thought for a moment, "traffic cams!" he said and pulled out his phone, "Officer Hoffman, 'I'm on the corner of 56th and 8th, I got a blue SUV heading south, I need a tail on him NOW! Hoffman snapped his phone shut. Hoffman insisted on staying old school, he had an old flip phone with a black and white screen. in his words 'It feels nicer to end a call with a slam shut then a tap on a screen' whatever. I called the station and requested a full surveillance on Arcane Abyss. I figured he might be heading the long way round and we might just catch him there, as I ended the call Hoffman received a message from the patrol car 'Hoffman we just lost him!' Hoffman swore under his breath, "damnit!" he pounded his fist on the wall. "How do we know it wasn't a gang member doing this?" I said, hoping to alleviate his anger. Hoffman shook his head in disbelief, he paused, like all the puzzle pieces scattering around his brain locked together in an instance. He pointed towards the alleyway we came from and smiled. "What?" I asked, "we just came from there!" Hoffman walked back into the alleyway. "Come on" he said as he continued walking "He ditched something, here" Hoffman pointed to the floor. "Chasing him, I didn't think anything of it. but now" Hoffman leaned down by some bushes "why wouldn't he want us catching him with this?" picking up a small orb off the ground. I leaned down and looked at it "what is it?" Hoffman looked at me and grinned. "This belongs to the electric dragonflies, they use it to capture and imprison victims".

V

Abara's Crucible

The room was dark, Abara felt groggy, his limbs were weak and heavy, his breath short and tiresome. He gained consciousness slowly, his body ached from being stretched to his limits, his muscles tensed, he realised that his hands and legs were tied to a metal chair. The room was small, a table with a chair opposite and a door on the left of the room. The room was windowless, the light came from a bare bulb hanging from the ceiling. He could hear a faint hum from an electrical outlet on the wall and he recognised the buzz of fluorescent lights. He shook his head in frustration, his vision blurred, and his mind racing. He tried to focus, to remember what happened and how he got here.

A large, imposing man entered the room, his skin scarred with thick deep welts, a jagged scar across his face. As the demon sat down on the chair opposite his figure changed, twitching back and forth into a demon. His face, hunched forward, with sharp curved teeth and glowing eyes. The demonic figure grabbed a cup of water off the table and put it to his lips, but before he could drink Abara's body tensed up and he shouted. "Who are you?!" The demon slammed the cup down onto the table with force. He glared at Abara with hate in his eyes, the light flickered. Within a split second the demon transformed into Samira before switching back to his monstrous form and snarling, taunting Abara, the demon confused him, snapping back and forth like an old light flickering in the darkness. He pointed his finger at Abara and grinned a most sinister grin, he was clearly enjoying the effect he was having.

The door swung open and a familiar voice rang out "Arrgh! Help Me!" Abara looked to the open door in shock "Samira! Samira? Where are you?" The demon jumped up from his chair and began to laugh, leaving Abara alone tied to the chair. the door slammed shut. Abara could hear Samira's voice echoing from the other side of the door. "What is this place?" Abara questioned to himself under his breath. He shouted in frustration "Samira!" he tugged on the ropes, trying to pull them free, but the bindings were too strong, he could not break free.

"Samira! Can you hear me? Please answer" He could hear muffled cries from beyond the door. "Samira, please tell me what's going on? Where are we? Samira? I'm here with you" Samira shouted, her voice filled with fear. "Abara! You're here!" She shouted back "thank god, help me!" she pleaded. "It's alright Samira, I'll get you out of here." Abara strained his body, pulling his wrists apart, trying to tear through the ropes that held him. Samira was crying now, "Abara! I'm scared!" Abara could not take it, he felt helpless, he didn't know what to do, he screamed out in desperation, tears pouring down his face. "I'm here, Samira! I'm going to get us out of here" he screamed, "I need you to stay calm and listen to me!"

Abara knew Samira well, she was smart, he knew that she would keep a clear head and think rationally to try and get them out of there. She knew that Abara was a great officer and that he was strong, he would protect her, and if they both worked together, they could find a way out of this place. Abara yelled towards Samira. "Samira, where are you? can you describe the room you're in?" he heard

Samira's voice faintly reply, "I'm in an interrogation room, with some sort of.." Samira stopped abruptly and screamed out. "AAARGH! NO NO NO PLEASE!" Samira cried in pain, followed by a thud, and then silence. Abara tugged on his bindings with all his strength, the chair broke free from the bolts holding Abara in place, his arms strained from the weight, the ropes snapped free "Samira, SAMIRA! I'm free, SAMIRA!" as he stood up, the demon laughed "Too late!"

Abara dashed to the door and tried to open it, but it was locked. He could hear a commotion from beyond the door, shouting and screaming. Samira's voice begged for help. "I'm here Samira, I'm not going to leave you, please hold on" Abara ran to the far end of the room, hoping to find something that could help him. He took a step back and charged shoulder first causing a loud smash, Abara escaped the room.
Abara sprinted down the corridor, the sound of the demon laughing haunted his mind. Abara burst through the door, shards and splinters flew in the air. His worst nightmare, Samira was strapped naked to a torture device. Her body was covered in blood and bruises, she was barely conscious, she looked up to see her captor, he was sitting on a stool, watching her suffer, enjoying the show. The demon laughed and looked at Abara, his voice changed, mimicking him "After all these years, you've forgotten me?" The demon reverted to his low raspy tone and continued to laugh, disappearing into dust, leaving Abara and Samira alone in the room. Abara rushed to Samira's side "Samira? Are you okay?" Samira slowly opened her

eyes and looked up at Abara. She smiled and whispered "I knew you would come." covered in blood and exhausted from the horrific act she had suffered, Abara could not help himself. He grabbed hold of her and pulled her close, her soft lips pressed up against his, her arms wrapped around his neck, the pain from her wounds all but forgotten as she surrendered to her urges. Samira pulled herself away from Abara in anger and glared at him, her eyes white and a fluorescent beam shone from her gaping mouth.

Abara felt weak, the energy drained from his body, he clambered backwards until his back hit the wall, his knees buckling, he slid down to the floor. He looked up at Samira, her body changing shape, the blood on her skin, her clothes torn and ripped. "Samira?" Abara called out weakly. Samira's body changed shape and colour, she grew long, sharp talons from her hands, her face became hideous with jagged teeth. Her body convulsed as her wings sprouted, fluttering to life. Samira flew into the air, screaming and cackling, she hovered around Abara and hissed. "You'll never be able to escape this place," Samira snarled. Abara looked up at Samira, tears falling from his eyes, he tried to talk, but was unable to form a sentence, "I'm sorry" Abara stammered "I was too late" Samira continued "you can't escape. not yet." her voice lowered, almost inaudible, "not yet..."

The room dimmed into darkness, Abara tried to see through the gloom, but nothing was visible. He heard voices from his past, screaming and wailing. The shadows faded, as light pierced the darkness.

Abara was in Azurite City, or so he thought. Confused, his head darted up and down the street, nobody to be seen, this was strange. Abara was opposite Pacific Grove Academy, it was the middle of the day and no one was around, no children in the playground, no teachers yelling, no one. Abara looked closely at the school, there was a strange figure banging on the front door. "Hello? Is anyone there? Abara started to run, he ran towards the front gates of the school and stood in an archway watching the figure. The figure looked up and turned around, he looked straight at Abara. His skin was pale, with black veins protruding from his body, he was thin, his eyes sunken. He looked frightened and confused. He opened his mouth to speak but Abara did not hear the words he tried to say. The strange man moved over towards an open window and climbed in. Abara followed, climbing through the window and into the building. The room was dark and cold, he followed the strange man into a corridor and then down a set of stairs. He had never seen this part of the school before, he was intrigued and wanted to know what the stranger was doing. Abara reached for his pistol but nothing was there, his hand went straight through the holster. "Wah!" Abara muttered to himself.

The strange man opened a door at the end of the corridor, it was locked and had a heavy duty padlock on the door handle. Abara caught up to him "Freeze! Don't move!" he shouted. The strange man looked up at Abara and smiled. "It's ok," he said, looking down at the padlock. He held out his hand and the padlock turned to ash and fell to the ground. Watching the padlock fall Abara took his eyes off the man, as he did the shadowing figure zoomed forward and a loud bang echoed through the hallway. Abara stepped back feeling a sharp punch, with the wind knocked out of him, he looked down at his stomach, his clothes had torn, his skin ripped and blood poured out.

The man stood over Abara, his fist bleeding from the impact. Abara's point of view changed in a flash, looking down at the body on the floor he could see his son, writhing in agony the voice of his son squealing in pain, just a boy, only seven years old. Abara's eyes widened in horror, he looked up at the attacker to see himself, only older. "How?" Abara screamed, in pain, his mind racing, his body wracked with shock and terror. Abara's eyes filled with tears as he watched his son's life fade away, his vision blurred as the room around him faded to black, leaving him alone in the void.

"H-help... me" Abara's voice weakened, he was fading in and out of reality, his head was pounding, he couldn't see or hear anything.

"There is a way out!" A voice softly broke the silence. Abara recognised the male voice immediately. "You will see that everything makes sense if you try hard enough." The voice was calming, reassuring, it spoke to him with empathy. Abara was confused, where was he? Was he dreaming? "Who are you? Where am I?" Abara questioned, his voice weak, but clear enough for the voice to hear.

"I need you Abara, but not as you are. I need; The real you!" The voice paused, giving Abara time to think. "I can show you how to get out of this place, but in order to do so you need to trust me." Abara contemplated the voice's offer. As he realised the madness of the situation, Samira's scream echoed through his mind, her face as she was strapped to the torture device, covered in blood and her clothes torn and ripped. "Or. I just leave you here?"

The faint sound of footsteps grew louder and louder, as they became louder the ground shook. A horde of creatures came to life around him, screeching and wailing, emerging from the ground, running toward Abara with such speed and ferocity. Abara looked around to find himself surrounded, there was no way out. It was the demonic figure from before, but this time hundreds of them, all clamouring around him, they circled him strategically before pouncing, one by one their claws ripped his body apart, their teeth gnashing at the air, as Abara dodged attacks, he was no match for them.

Abara could feel himself changing, his skin hardened and became warm, his muscles growing with each second, Abara's face deformed and morphed into a hideous being, his eyes bright and glowing. He opened his mouth to speak, but his jaw was too big for his mouth, he could not form words, instead he growled, he took a deep breath in, arched his back and pointed his face upwards panting like a dog, Abara gave a monstrous howl. The floor beneath him began to crack and tear apart, the demons vanished, Abara felt himself being pulled back, like the undercurrent of a river. The curse lifted, the beast rose and was greeted by Pavlov. Pavlov's plan was coming to form.

VI

The Beast of Azurite City

The years that followed Abara's disappearance were dark, crime rose due to the lack of leadership. The police were unable to stop the onslaught of violence, with more victims appearing every day. The city seemed to be collapsing. The government had to re-implement the emergency laws, Lock-downs and curfews were in place for all citizens of Azurite City. The streets became as dangerous as a warzone, rival gangs fought for territory. The death toll reached over five hundred. The bodies were piled up like sacks of flour. The people were scared to go out in fear of being robbed, beaten up, or worse, killed. One creature was always to blame, as its infamy rose, people would refer to it as The Beast of Azurite City.

Pavlov's rise to power came with the threat of his most powerful weapon in the form of the weaponized Canine Pithovirus. The virus had the ability to cause a violent frenzy, the infected would turn into mindless beasts with the sole purpose of destroying everything in sight, pure and ultimate rage. The death toll rose by the day, the citizens became afraid of their own shadow. Most of the citizens decided to leave the city in search of a better life, a safer life elsewhere, leaving the thousands of victims behind. Pavlov rose in popularity due to his ability to quell the infected with a simple shot, after all he created the virus. With this power, he could control the citizens with ease. The rich and the powerful reluctantly befriended Pavlov ensuring their survival, this was his plan all along, a criminal underworld that he ruled, with nobody to stop him. The Beast of Azurite City at his side, Pavlov ruled the city with fear, but only for a while...

The beast began to act on its own accord, Its exposure to the virus took its toll and each year Abara faded and the beast took over, Pavlov did not account for this. The beast was like a wild animal, it's true nature was to destroy, his intelligence was animalistic. One late evening the beast snuck into Pavlov's compound, its stealthy nature made short work of the guards on duty. In rage the beast attacked Pavlov, scarring his face permanently. Pavlov scrambled to the floor in shock, his face covered in blood, this only enticed the beast more. The sweet sticky smell of blood imbued the beast with a savage urge. As it slowly approached, Pavlov trembled in fear, he begged for his life, pleading, hoping that Abara was still inside. Pavlov promised to give him anything he wanted. But the Beast did not want his empty promises, it only wanted to rip out his throat. Pavlov, always the cunning worlock, sprang to his feet with a handful of green powder in hand, he took a deep breath, smiled and blew hard into the beast's face. As the dust flew, it began to convulse, thrash about and collapse on the floor, convulsing, its body burned with a green glow. The beast grew quiet as its skin melted away, leaving not a beast but a whimpering dog. "stupid dog!" Pavlov cocked his hand back and stuck the dog, smacking its face. Pavlov grabbed it's chin and pointed it's face toward him "look what you did to me!" Pavlov screamed, he paused then displayed a sinister grin "Nothing compared to Samira, ay" the dog looked up at him, his eyes widened in sadness. Pavlov could see, Abara was still in there.

Pavlov settled down, conducting business at his nightclub he never really left the Arcane Abyss. Past citizens slowly regained their homes and Azurite City began to rise back up, the city was once again full of life and hope. The beast attacking Pavlov had an effect, it was the start of a new chapter in Pavlov's life, one, not of anger and violence, but one where he could dabble in business whilst letting the pawns get in trouble. there was still evil in his future, but a different kind of evil.

VII

Break the Fast

Hoffman and I always hit this spot on the 10th, 'Break the fast'. Red and white leather booths ran along the large windows overlooking the city, and a large bar separated the kitchen from the booths. Little padded stools were tucked under the bar, it never got too busy to find a seat. That greasy spoon served the best Chicken pot pie, perfect crust on top with a hearty filling and a rich creamy gravy on the side. If I could have only one meal till the day I died it would be a chicken pot pie from Break the fast; perfection. Hoffman always had the all day breakfast or the 'All day Break the fast' as they called it, thick cuts of streaky bacon, two smoky cajun sausages, a mountain of beans, mushrooms and scrambled eggs and two tomatoes, Hoffman always added black pudding too. To this day I'm always shocked at how skinny he is.

We entered the diner, considering it being around six in the evening, Break the fast was dead. Just two old cops at the end of the bar sipping black coffees, probably on shift. I flagged the waitress, holding my hand up "Usuals please Stace" We sat at our normal booth adjacent to the windows, Hoffman rubbed his forehead and squeezed his eyes "Right! Girl, mid twenties, found by residents in the same building" I continued "Tied to that…thing, naked, marks all over body and signs she'd been there for some time." Hoffman nodded and replied " Apartment, empty and a.." Hoffman paused before continuing "Worlocks cursed symbol on her wrist" I looked at Hoffman, "Pavlov claims he has no idea about the mark or the girl" "And we have no proof" Hoffman clenching his fist whilst churning words through his teeth.

I quickly carried on, trying to divert Hoffman's attention from Pavlov. "Unknown suspect seen at crime scene fleeing apartment, dropping an orb, only used by the electric dragonflies" Hoffman concluded "And the dragonflies haven't been seen together for years"

"One chicken pot pie, extra gravy and one All day 'Break the fast' scrambled eggs with two black puddings. Can I get any drinks for ya?"

I was too engrossed in the case files, I didn't even see the waitress at our table place the food in front of me. Hoffman replied "Two coffees, one black, no sugar. One white two sugars, Thank you" Hoffman turned to me, "You thinking about Nyx?" I sighed and just shrugged my shoulders "Yeah"

"Listen, Ant. we'll find out who did this, we always do" Hoffman rarely used my first name, only when the time felt appropriate I suppose.

The waitress came back with our coffees and a pot of sugar. "Enjoy fellas" I looked at her, she was stunningly beautiful, perfect body, blonde curly hair and blue eyes. I realised I was staring, I took a mouthful of coffee and started to feel the heat spread across my face.

I could hear the waitress whispering to the cook behind the kitchen doors, I couldn't quite make it out but I was sure she said something like,

"God damn he's cute, young ones not bad either"

Hoffman gave me a look, I ignored it, he knew I was taken with her. Hoffman coughed and went back to the case, it wasn't something he was going to let drop anytime soon.

As the night progressed, the diner slowly filled with more people. The music in the diner was slow and relaxed, perfect for a mid-week meal out. I looked around the diner, I noticed the two old cops we saw on the way in, they seemed to be chatting and laughing like they were old friends. It was interesting, what was their story, how long did they serve on the force? They looked a little like Hoffman and I, only thirty years older. Imagine the stories and cases they've been through. I loved to watch people, maybe the detective in me, maybe I'm just nosey, cooking up stories, lives and relationships gave me a warm fuzzy feeling inside. It distracted me from the horrors of the job.

Hoffman took one bite of his beans and Cajun sausage and moaned with pleasure. He's such a sucker for junk food, I mean seriously, the amount he put in his mouth and the speed he devoured them, I'm amazed he still had time to breathe. I let him enjoy his meal as I poked at mine, normally both our chins would be glued to the table, conversation halted to silence, but this case was personal, I needed revenge, but on who?

As Hoffman chased the last mushrooms off his plate, it came to me "Alyssa!" Hoffman looked up "what!?" I learned in making sure we couldn't be heard "Alyssa Reed, from our days at the precinct. she worked closely with the rehabilitation of addicts tied to the faction war, surely she'd know more about Worlocks and the orbs" Hoffman took a sip of coffee,

"Alright, let's call it a night, we'll drive over tomorrow morning. pay a visit." I reached in my back pocket and grabbed my wallet, ruffling through bills, I flagged the waitress "Thanks" placing the notes under my coffee cup we left the diner, I took one last look at the waitress as I left, her eyes met mine for a brief moment, it felt like the room was filled with electricity.

We got into the car, the engine purred to life and we set off in the direction of my place. My place was Immaculate, stainless steel worktops with oak accents, glasswork sculptures adorned the lounge, and my bed was covered in down pillows and sheets. I kept my apartment in a perfect state, just in case I had...visitors. "Right pal, catch ya tomorrow" I stepped out of the car and walked up to my apartment door, it had been a long day, so much had happened, the girl in that contraption, the arcane abyss, the diner.

I walked over to the kitchen and poured myself a whiskey, with Hoffman not around I could comfortably drink without worrying about triggering his addiction issues. Glenmorangie Single Malt Scotch Whisky, I took a large mouthful and made my way to the bathroom.

Turning on the shower, steam began to rise as I undressed. I stood and looked at myself in the mirror. My eyes were bloodshot, my body and face were covered in scars, some from my time on the force and some from my bare knuckle boxing days. I knew I was a handsome man, but that only made the scars all the more painful. I turned around to examine my back, an angry scar from a bullet wound, a blade to the side and the exit wound scar was still pink, I've never been able to get rid of it, I looked like a walking corpse

The warm water washed away the dirt and grime of the day. I lay in bed, thoughts of the day were flooding my head, slowly my eyes began to feel heavy, eventually I drifted off. My phone rang, I had set it to silent mode, but it rang again. "For fuck sake" I said out loud, I sat up in bed and reached over for my phone. "What the fuck is this about?" I looked at the Caller ID 'Doc H' I grinned and texted back "yeah, come over"

I got out of bed and poured two glasses of wine, the doc lived only five minutes away, I knew she wouldn't be long. The doorbell rang, I opened the door naked "exactly what the doctor ordered" She chuckled and bit her lip as she pounced on me and pushed me into the apartment

She straddled me and moved her hips to grind into my body, I loved this woman, she had been there for me more times than I cared to remember, she was perfect, she knew everything about me, and I knew everything about her, we knew each other's bodies like our own, every mark, scar, inch of skin, we knew it all.

We moved violently around the apartment, I made love to her on the kitchen table, she fucked me in the shower, the kitchen, the lounge, the bathroom, my bed. My phone rang constantly, it was probably Hoffman, but we were enjoying ourselves too much. We collapsed on the bed, completely spent. "It's been a while Liv?" I asked in between breaths, she rested her head on my shoulder. "Too long, I'm just glad you're here" she replied "So am I" I lay on my side and pulled Liv close to me. "I've missed you" She rolled over to face me "You know I'm always here, Ant." She pulled me closer, and kissed me softly "I know, but I need you more now than I've ever needed you before" She kissed me again, our tongues locked, I rolled over on top of her, she opened her mouth and pushed her tongue into mine, her hands exploring my body. I reached up to her face and pulled her towards me, kissing her neck and down her chest. My tongue flicked her nipple, slowly working down her body until she was panting with anticipation. Her breathing increased and I felt her hand pulling my hair. "I've missed you, babe" She let out a loud moan as my tongue found its mark.

I lifted my head, she pushed me back and moved to straddle me again. Slowly she lowered herself onto me, her hips began to tremble, I looked up at her, I felt her orgasm approaching. She came violently, her body bucking as she screamed my name. She lay on me panting "Oh my God!" she gasped "that was incredible!" She collapsed next to me.

We both lay on the bed in silence, just enjoying each other's company.

Liv put her hand on my chest "I'm sorry Ant...about Nyx" I pulled her close, kissing her forehead. "Me too, She was a good guardian" I thought about it, Nyx *was* a good guardian, and a great warrior, she did her job but, it shouldn't have ended the way it did, I could feel tears welling up, but I swallowed them and smiled before falling asleep with Liv in my arms.

VIII

Old Friends

The next day I woke up before Liv. I decided to take a shower before she woke up. Stepping into the warm water washed away thoughts of the previous day. My phone was ringing, it was probably Hoffman. I turned to face the shower head and rinsed the shampoo out of my hair. Liv joined me in the shower, I loved the feeling of her soft skin against mine, she lathered up the suds and caressed our bodies. Soft jazz played in the background, she must have turned on the radio before coming in. I wanted her, I wanted her badly, couldn't we have just taken the day off? Thoughts raced my mind as the scent of wild jasmine filled the apartment.

The water felt good against my skin, I rinsed off and stepped out of the shower. "Where are you going?" Liv asked as I dried myself "Hoffman will be here soon, going to visit Alyssa about the case" Liv looked at me, I knew exactly what she was going to say, "Be careful out there Ant. promise me." I looked back at her and smiled "always. Croque Madame? cinnamon latte?" Liv grinned "you know me so well" I left the apartment to get some breakfast, The little french bakery three doors down, served the best pastries, Liv loved the Croque Madame, she had it everytime. Chloe worked behind the counter, she served me every day, short stocky women, spoke in a deep husky voice and loved her food. Chloe always greeted me with a smile, as I walked in she could tell I was in a good mood, the stupid grin on my face gave it away. *"Oh, regarde ça, ton sourire est positivement radieux!"* I had no idea what she said, but by the look on her face, she was happy to see me, service was swift here, perfect, I wanted to get back to Liv as soon as possible. I reckon this sucker had fallen in love…again.

"Liv!" I shouted as I entered the apartment, Liv popped her head round the corner, she looked immaculate, "there you are" she replied with a smirk, I could tell she was already missing me "Breakfast is served" I replied, she made her way to the kitchen and started laying out plates.

I went into my room and got dressed. A crisp black shirt, tan slacks and a baby blue suit jacket...perfect. Breakfast in each other's company was utter bliss and exactly what I needed, we didn't need chit-chat, we were two people who had been through hell and back together.

As we finished up breakfast, the shrill sound of the front doorbell rang. I left Liv to tidy the dishes as I went to answer the door. "Hoffman, come in" As Hoffman entered I grinned as he clocked Liv, "Oh! Doc, you're here!" Hoffman said in shock as he walked in. "You two back on then?" Liv laughed, "Not quite" She grinned as she walked towards the door, she looked down looking a little shy before looking back at me "But we'll see how it goes"

"You be safe Ant" She kissed me and left, her perfume blissfully lingered. Hoffman gave a '*We both know where this leads*' look. "Right! I'll meet you in the car, gotta grab a few things" I gestured over to the mess in the corner, Hoffman laughed. Piles of paperwork dog-eared and lumped together, somehow I knew where everything was, even if it looked like a dump "sure thing" Hoffman walked out of my apartment swinging his car keys, fiddling with the keyfob.

I got in the car expecting a full lecture about keeping work and personal life separate, but Hoffman kept his cool, never mentioned it once. "I gave Alyssa a heads up, she knows we're coming," Hoffman said, glancing at the clock on the car dashboard, "should be about an hour, give or take, depending on traffic" Traffic leaving the city was always a nightmare, never as bad as coming in. Maybe there's something in that, who knows.

The stark contrast between Azurite city and the suburbs was almost like two different worlds. The houses here had much larger lots. I could even see a few forested areas among them, the city was crammed, dirty and had a strange sweet pungent smell like ripe fruit. The Suburbs however were clean, open and smelt like the pine needles.

We were making our way to the new business district, just past the suburbs. President Alyssa worked in a tall office building that looked over all of the surrounding areas, which was great. Azurite City looked stunning from afar, a sprawling metropolis located on the west coast, The city was divided into several distinct districts, each with its own unique characteristics and challenges, opulence and luxury, with extravagant shopping malls, high-end restaurants, and luxurious apartments.

We pulled up to the front gate to be greeted by the security officer working the barrier. A rather large man dressed in a suit, his black hair tied into a tight bun on top of his head, he smiled as we pulled up.

"Good morning" he said to me in a kind, slow voice, "do you have an appointment?" He asked politely.

"appointment? no but President Alyssa is an old friend and she is expecting us" I replied in the same manner, my grandpa always used to say '*you get more bees with Honey*'. My grandpa worked a twelve hour shift construction job six days a week for fifty-two years, always came home smiling, always taught us to treat people with dignity and respect, I learned alot from him, I miss him dearly.

The security guard's smile turned to a frown, he checked the tablet in front of him, scrolling his finger repeatedly.

"Ahh, yes... it's in the note section, my apologies fellas. one sec" The guard reached over and pushed the buzzer. The gates opened in a slow swinging motion "Cheers pal" Hoffman nodded "Av a good one"

The drive towards the office building was long, immaculate shrubbery on both sides with a lush green lawn, the grounds were kept very well. There was no doubt about it.

Hoffman parked the vehicle outside the building and looked up at the gleaming structure. The building itself looked like it was made from some kind of metallic glass, with silver lines running across it like veins. It looked almost futuristic.

"This place is a lot bigger than I thought" I scanned the building from the ground floor to the top. Stepping out of the car we both took a second to admire the sheer size and exquisite design of the building. Hoffman whistled "shit that's big"

As we approached the front door Alyssa greeted us in the lobby, "You two haven't aged a day" she then glanced at Hoffman "Well you, maybe" We both laughed, Hoffman grinned trying to hold back a chuckle.

Alyssa was still as beautiful as ever, she wore a white collared shirt with a black suit skirt, her black curly hair bounced as she walked, Her smile was warm and genuine, "Follow me, I'll take you up to my office" she said, motioning to the lift. "We can chat up there, in private"

The elevator was enormous, large enough to fit several people comfortably. The walls had a mirror finish and overlooked the grounds below, stereotypical elevator music softly played in the background as the doors shut, Alyssa pushed a blank button and pressed her thumb to the scanner. Alyssa was definitely flexing, either that or my jealousy was raging, fancy secret offices in a swanky art deco building was no comparison to the rundown precinct Hoffman and I clocked in everyday. The doors closed, the car started moving upwards in an instant, "How long has it been?" Alyssa asked. "Almost ten years, give or take" I replied "But I've seen you on the news, you're a big name now"

She smiled and looked down at the floor, "Thank you, it's been hard work" she said with a little sigh, "The last ten years have been full of surprises, we had no idea how badly we were underfunded"

We came to a halt and the doors opened "My office is this way, please make yourself comfortable" Alyssa led the way to her office.

We were on the top floor, with a stunning view of the entire city. She sat down on a chair behind a desk, opposite where we stood.

"Well, I'm glad you guys are here," she laughed. "you both look like you've been through hell"

I responded, "That's kinda why we're here"

Alyssa nodded, her expression turning serious "Alright, what do you need?"

"We're looking for someone," Hoffman replied.

Alyssa's face was confused for a moment. "Ok, who?"

Hoffman looked back to me, I took a deep breath and exhaled slowly. "by now you must have heard about the young girl, in her 20's, found dead, rigged up to a torture device?"

Alyssa's expression dropped and she nodded her head, "Yeah, horrific"

"You could say that" I responded, as I handed over a folder of evidence. Alyssa opened it, quickly flicking through the contents, her face turning grim, as her eyes scanned the papers inside. "Jesus," she muttered under her breath.

"It's a lot to take in, so I'll just put it plainly, we suspect Pavlov, but we can't pin him on anything" I sighed.

"Worlocks curse!" Alyssa stood up as she flicked through the pictures "The electric dragonflies left this mark on their victims all the time" She said, pointing at the picture.

"I know" I replied "And I know that they are long gone, but I suspect he has a network"

Alyssa stopped at a picture of the victim's face "....doesn't she.." she whispered.

"What's that?" Hoffman asked, stepping towards the desk.

Alyssa turned around and passed him the folder "Look at her, there's something familiar about her"

Hoffman looked at the photo for a long time as Alyssa moved her computer mouse to wake up the screens, "Over here!" she said, pointing at the computer.

I looked up at the screens, there was a photo of a group of people, they were standing outside a building. The photo was a little blurry and grainy but I could see the lettering above them 'ACPD'. Alyssa pointed at one of the faces "Look! Captain Samira!" I gasped "It can't be"

"Captain Samira died around the same time Sergeant Abara went missing" Alyssa's eyes widened in shock, she maximised an image from the evidence folder.

"Fuck Me!" Hoffman gasped, I turned to see a close up of the young woman, same angle, same device, same markings. "But if she died then, it couldn't have been Samira again?"

Alyssa frantically moved windows around the desktop of her computer, "No, but she did have a daughter ... .Mira, she would be in her twenties and look!" Alyssa flagged a yearbook profile of Mira who looked just like victim

"so, the killer is targeting women that fit the same profile, but why?" Hoffman pondered out loud whilst pacing around the room.

The abrupt interruption of ringtones disrupted our thought process, both Hoffman and I looked at our phones, he had a call, mine was a message. I remember Hoffman once roasted a young detective for sending him a text message about a case, it was in an abbreviated format which only made sense if you knew and used it regularly. He shouted at that kid for a solid thirty minutes, spittle flying everywhere. I couldn't decide if I felt bad for the kid or enjoyed the silliness of it all, sure made an impression on the precinct though, nobody would dare send him a text now.

Hoffman put his phone to his ear, "Hello? What! I'm on my way" he ended the call "We've got him, another murder, same device!" He turned to me, I could see the agitation on his face.

"Not another!" I sighed "Let's go!" I looked back to Alyssa, "Thank you for your help"

"It's no problem, if you have any more questions or evidence, please call." she smiled, "You take care now!" she called out as Hoffman and I headed back towards the lift.

"It's strange" Hoffman pondered, "Why would Pavlov be killing off Samira's family? Or women who looked like her? What's the link?"

The lift door opened and we walked out into the lobby.

"I'm not sure, but if we find that link, it will lead us to Pavlov, and then we can finally get some justice" I sighed as we exited the building. The car was waiting for us outside. I hopped in the passenger side as Hoffman followed me and jumped in the driver's seat.

IX

The Killer strikes again

Hoffman sped across the city, the sounds of gunfire and explosions getting louder and louder as he drove. When we arrived at the city's edge, Hoffman brought the vehicle to a screeching halt, Huge crowds blocked the roads as they fled the city, trying to get to safety.

The S.W.A.T truck stopped near us, Four officers jumped out from the back and ran into the crowds. I waved Hoffman over to follow as I ran out towards the crowd, Squad cars surrounded an old factory building, there were no lights and the factory looked like it was abandoned, half broken windows boarded up, the roof looked like it was going to collapse. The factory certainly wasn't in use, thank god.

"Costa!, is that you? Is Hoffman with you?" an officer in front asked as he ran to meet us.

"Yes, were you first on the scene? what happened?" I asked as I caught my breath.

"We found another" the officer could barely get his words out "In the basement, same torture device, same scars, but we've cornered a man fleeing the scene, he has a kid with him and they're hiding in the abandoned factory, we're trying to negotiate a surrender"

"What about the victim? alive?" I asked, almost afraid of the answer.

"No, sir. What that animal did to her, she had no chance. It's Fuckin' brutal"

"Fuck!" I screamed, rubbing my forehead. Hoffman just caught up, "What'd I miss?" I turned to Hoffman shaking my head "Another victim, same way, same device"

"Jesus Costa," Hoffman said quietly, his eyes wide.

One of the S.W.A.T officers approached us, "We've got a hostage situation, need a negotiator. You two are the most senior officers on site" She looked at us with a blank stare, waiting for an answer.

"Okay, I'll talk to him" I said nodding to Hoffman and walking towards the entrance to the factory, S.W.A.T officers handed me a bulletproof vest, this made me nervous, something about a clunky vest made me think of tempting the inevitable, like I'm going to get shot, but I'll be wearing this bulky vest so it'll just be a bruise, I can add to the patch work of scars i've already accumulated.

I walked up to the factory door, one of the S.W.A.T officers let me inside. It was dark, the factory had only one solitary light coming from a single bulb in the middle of the room, shadows plagued every inch of the room. "Hello!" I shouted, my voice echoed around the room, I could hear a gun being cocked. "I'm here to help you"

"NO CLOSER!" He shouted with authority but had a slight tremble at the end. He fired a warning shot and the light bulb shattered to the ground. The room quickly fell to darkness, I held my breath as glass flew around the room, I scrambled for cover behind a wooden table, hoping he couldn't see me.

"Look I can help you" I tried again, trying to keep my voice calm. "My name is Antonio Costa, I'm a detective,"

"Shut up!" The gunman shouted again.

I looked under the table and saw a child, he was shaking, terrified. "Do you have a kid with you?" I asked, trying to get him to talk.

"Stay away, or I'll blow his brains out!"

"OK, OK" I stayed crouched, holding my hands in the air, making sure he could see them. "I'm not here to hurt you"

"Just...just stay back."

"Okay, okay, I'm not going to come any closer" All I could think of was the safety of that kid.

"I'm gonna stay here, my arms in the air. You're in charge pal. But I guarantee if he gets hurt" I gestured slowly to the kid " S.W.A.T outside will barge in regardless of me here, we both lose. so let's just chat ay"

There was a long pause, "ch...ch.chat, yeah, chat. I can do that"

I got up and started to walk to the side of the room, trying to keep the man talking, but making sure to keep my distance.

"So what's your name? What are you doing here?"

"What do you care? You're just another one of those cops aren't you? Just another goddamn pig. My father was a cop, so good that did him!" I could hear the gun shaking in his hands.

"Look, I just want to help you, why are you here? Do you know what happened here?" I pointed over to the room where the victim sat, strapped in the device.

"Yeah, I know. I know exactly what happened. I killed her, bu..but nothing happened, why, didn't anything happen"

"What do you mean noth-" I was cut short as he fired his gun again.

"GET BACK!" he could tell I was creeping toward him, he wanted to keep me at a distance.

I ducked behind the table again. "Let's start off with a name, ay?" I said with a friendly smile, trying to keep him talking, keep him from doing something…stupid

He sighed "Adil, My name is.." He stood up and kicked the boy towards me, the boy ran to me and hugged my side, "Shhhh, go. I want you to run towards those doors, don't look back!" I whispered to the boy, He ran as quick as he could, I waved to Hoffman through the gap in the door and turned to face the gunman

"My name is Adil Abara!" The gunman raised his pistol and aimed it directly at me, "ABARA!?" I reached for my guns, and pulled the trigger simultaneously. Catching him in the shoulder, He stumbled backwards and fired a few shots wildly before collapsing to the ground. I walked up to Adil, holding my gun to his forehead, my heart was beating hard, sweat pouring off my forehead, my hands shook from the adrenaline racing through my body. I took one deep breath and slowly exhaled through pursed lips.

"No more,"

I holstered my pistols and let S.W.A.T arrest him, they cuffed him and placed him in the back of a squad car before the paramedics came out. I turned to the S.W.A.T officer who spoke with me, "Where's the kid? the one with the gunman?"

"He ran through that door." The officer obliviously pointed to a door on the other side of the room.

"Oh Shit!" I ran over to the door and pushed it open, and the boy was kneeling by the victim, covered in blood. I ran to him, "Hey, you okay kid?" I placed my hand on his shoulder, "You okay?"

The boy slowly looked up at me, "Is she dead? Is my Mum Dead?"

"I'm sorry kid, she's gone" I pulled the boy's arm towards me and lifted him up, he hugged me tight and sobbed. Days like this made me question why I did this job, I didn't help that boy, not really. Such a small innocent child had his whole world turned upside down, we arrived after the horrific event, what was the point? The only thing I could offer him was justice, making sure this psychopath went down and served real time was my only goal. Justice for both of them.

I carried him out the building so forensics could collect evidence. I muttered under my breath "He'll pay!" As I walked out, I placed the boy down on the floor outside the factory and crouched to his level.

"What's your name, kid?"

He sniffled a bit as he tried to get a hold of himself, "George"

"That's a nice name" I wiped away some of the blood on his cheek and stood up, "do you know anyone that can come and collect you?"

George noded "I live with my aunt and uncle, my...my mum lives with us"

I took my phone out of my pocket and dialled a number "Can you bring a squad car round, I've got the kid, he needs a ride back home, we'll go through the case tomorrow" The squad car was only around the corner, so it only took seconds to get to us, a female patrol officer exited the vehicle, she looked at me and tilted her head toward him, I nodded and let him go with her. I waved to Hoffman before I walked back into the factory.

The forensic team were already in the building, some were putting a tarp over the device while others were collecting evidence, so I walked into the room where the victim was. The room was covered in blood, it was everywhere. The victim was still strapped to the chair, her mouth was covered by duct tape, she was still, but her eyes were wide open. I walked up to the device and saw the same symbols as the other two crime scenes, all I could do was cry, I couldn't bear to see someone like this. Hoffman pulled me aside "It's late pal, let's call it, forensics will finish here, we can question that psycho in the morning, c'mon" He patted my shoulder as he walked away, leaving me alone with the body.

I leaned against the wall and slid to the ground, holding my head in my hands. The adrenaline wore off and left me emotional, tears uncontrollably ran down my face. I needed air so I decided to walk home alone. "Hoffman!" I called "I'm gonna walk home, clear my head, I'll see ya tomorrow" Hoffman nodded and smiled as he got into his car.

Memories of Nyx flooded my mind, the cases we solved together, the battles we won, a sad and painfull end. I'd underestimated how far the old factory was from my place, I must have walked for half an hour and realised I wasn't even half way, so I hailed a cab, I hoped the driver didn't notice all the blood, that would have been hard to explain. We pulled up just in front of my apartment building "fourteen-ninety five" extortion! I had no other choice but to pay, cabs in this city were thieves. First thing I needed was a stiff drink. Had a little whisky left so I necked that down, the warm burn soothed the pain, before I knew it I was out cold.

Halfway through the night I checked my phone, a text message from Hoffman said that the gunman was at the police station. Interrogation started at 10. The exhaustion took over, maybe a little help from the whisky too, my eyes became heavy and I drifted back to sleep.

X

The Sins of the son

Sgt Abara's sudden disappearance took a toll on his son, with Captain Samira murdered there was nobody to raise Adil. Child protection services were forced to place Adil into foster care, the foster system in Azurite City was lacking to say the least. This was evident by the foster care that Adil received. An alcoholic and drug abuser and a sex worker somehow were granted sole custody of another life, they couldn't even take care of themselves nevermind a troubled young boy. His foster parents saw Adil as a paycheck. It was then that the nightmares truly began. He would wake up at night, screaming, crying, his foster parents just added to the screaming to get him to stop. When the frustration took over they beat him senseless, over and over, taking aggression out on the poor boy. Adil's life continued in this manner for 3 months.

It was around this time that Adil would begin to find some solace in the kindness of his fellow foster siblings. Some of the children would sneak away at night to Arcane Abyss. The bouncers at the door were told to ignore their ages and let them in, Pavlov's plan was to groom them into soldiers 'for the cause' Adil would tag along with them some nights. His confidence would always shine outside the foster home, he felt powerful, he felt like a leader. His group of friends became his brothers and sisters. They would sneak off to play games, tell stories, and explore the strange new criminal world, with Pavlov to guide them, they were unstoppable.

It was at the age of thirteen that Adil realised his talent for illusionism, Pavlov gave him a cheap pair of contact lenses that allowed him to see the aetheric spectrum, where all magical energies existed. Pavlov taught him how to manipulate his aetheric signature to avoid detection from most spell-casters. Adil came to love the art of making objects appear and disappear from sight, in reality, he was able to create illusions and teleport objects around him, but this ability would be hidden from others for many years.

When Adil turned fifteen, the other children stopped visiting Arcane Abyss, Adil began to spend more time there with Pavlov alone. He would sneak away from the orphanage, claiming that he was going out to meet friends, no one really cared any way. Pavlov recruited Adil into his criminal enterprise, making him an apprentice, learning all the ins and outs of the business, and began teaching him how to build the magical items he needed. Adil learned how to enchant magical items which led him to learn about the orbs that took hold of his father. Adil was now a key instrument to Pavlov's rise, however when Pavlov stopped his violent crimes, Adil continued, he became obsessed with power and knowledge. He knew that his father was tied to these magical orbs and somehow was trapped inside one. He wanted nothing more than to know the truth. He began to hunt down anyone and anything related to the orbs. Pavlov warned him not to get involved, but Adil didn't listen.

It was a month ago that Adil had found a clue to his father's whereabouts. A dark market dealer was selling a book written in a language that he did not understand. Adil decided to infiltrate the dark market dealer's store and steal the book from him, unable to read it he approached one of his brothers at the foster home. Together they translated each chapter of the book, one by one, growing in knowledge and power. *'Chapter XVII : Tying two souls together'*, This was where his questions were finally answered. The book described the ritual of two souls being bound together through the magical artefact known as the 'Soul Orb', a small spherical object that housed a soul trapped within it, the process had to be completed with a terrifying act, the death of a loved one. Adil read on frantically, he became obsessed, until Pavlov caught him and took the book from him, Pavlov was not pleased and took this as an act of betrayal, However Pavlov was too late, Adil learned of the location of the orbs.

Adil knew what he had to do, he had to find his father's orb. He had to know the truth, and nothing would get in his way. With the book now in Pavlov's hands Adil didn't have all the details, but began to develop his own theories. Was Captain Samira's death and his father's disappearance linked? Was the magic linked to their love for each other? Could he free his father by sacrificing another?

Adil stalked women that fit a certain profile, Brunettes with an athletic build, a slight hispanic look and exuded confidence, they looked just like Captain Samira. He never struck the confidence to approach, always observed from afar. Adil was unaware of Captain Samira's personal life, after all Abara and her had only been dating for a short time and the relationship was kept a secret, for professional reasons.

Adil met Mira by accident, Mira was training at the gym one night, she had just completed her workout and was stretching, Adil was a member of the same gym for sometime and became infatuated by her striking resemblance to Samira, he approached Mira and asked her out, to his surprise Mira agreed, they went on a date. Adil was obsessed with Mira, they continued dating for a while until Adil showed signs of controlling behaviour, insisting on knowing her whereabouts at all times, checking her phone, questioning her friends and calling to check up on her. Mira would beg him to stop but Adil would always refuse, Mira knew that something was wrong but was unaware of the fact that Adil was plotting her demise, Adil wanted to kill Mira to release his father's soul.

Adil had planned Mira's death for months now, he had been waiting for the perfect moment. On Mira's birthday, Adil snuck into her apartment and removed all the furniture. The living room, kitchen and bedroom were all gutted empty, he carefully rigged the terrifying machine in the centre of the room, it was a combination of wires, pipes and drills that connected to an electrical lever, Adil planned on torturing Mira to death, he was adamant that this would sever the link between the two souls, that he would free his father. Adil was in the process of testing the machine when Mira arrived home from her evening jog. Mira saw what Adil had done and was terrified. Adil immediately rushed to Mira, begging her to not move, pleading with her. Mira looked into Adil's eyes, In desperation, tears began to roll down her face. Adil began to weep, the sound of his father's voice filled his mind screaming for help.

Adil made up his mind, he knew he had to kill Mira to save his father. He pushed her to the ground and knocked her unconscious. Adil stripped Mira naked and rigged her to the machine, carefully placing her body into the contraption, as he clipped the last clasp that held her head in place, gripping onto her hair, she awoke, dazed, disorientated, muttering desperate words. Adil stared into her eyes and pulled the lever. Mira screamed in agony as the machine cut through her skin, ripping her to shreds, her body twisted, spasmed and gushed blood. The machine roared to life, as it vivisected her body, tearing her to pieces, blood poured from her wounds. Adil was unaware of Mira's healing abilities, as the machine overpowered and cut out, Mira's wounds healed, not fully though, deep scars formed as her skin closed together. In shock Adil looked at the metre on the machine, 98%. Adil pulled the lever again, he couldn't stop, over and over he pulled that lever until she finally gave in. Mira's body collapsed and slumped over, lifeless. Adil waited over Mira's body, unable to speak, the sight of Mira's mutilated body terrified him. The sight of her blood pooling on the floor made him nauseous. "FUCK!" Adil expected to feel something, an indication that it worked. Nothing. Overwhelmed, Adil ran out of the apartment, in the commotion dropping an orb onto the floor. Adil ran out into the street sobbing, in shock, and in disbelief, unable to process what he had done.

XI

Interrogation

It was 9:15 and I was dressed, ready for the day, evidence raced through my mind as I remembered the case, the poor victims and their families, that little boy. His life changed forever. I walked over to the precinct, I planned how the interrogation would go, certain plays Hoffman and I had were guaranteed to go our way, the good cop, bad cop routine was a cliche and didn't work. Hoffman liked to pay attention to what the suspect wasn't saying, microaggressions and twitches told a whole new side of what really happened, me? I didn't have the patience for all that, I usually took charge, yelled at them till they cried the truth.

I entered through the double doors and continued toward my office, my desk was covered with papers. I stood and looked around, Spending time on the streets took me away from the manic rush of officers in the bullpen. I missed it, it seemed like I hadn't seen it in months. Deeply engrossed in paperwork, the faint calling from Hoffman got louder and louder. Finally, he caught my attention, "Got a little something for ya pal". I was a little disappointed when I saw a simple manila folder with a few papers in it, it was the evidence from the crime scene the night before. Forensics placed Adil all over the scene, fingerprints, DNA even his shoe treads, an exact match to the sneakers he had on, the only thing we needed was motive.

We headed over to the interrogation room, the two rooms were separated by a one way mirror, we entered the observation room first, Officer Jacobs sat there reading the AC times. The AC times was the city's number one newspaper, filled with local gossip and celebrity nonsense. I hated the press and the garbage drivel they printed.

He turned to us and nodded. "Morning detectives." as he ruffled the paper and folded it away pretending to do his job.

Hoffman smiled, shaking his head. "Mornin' Jacobs, how's it going?" Jacobs was a short man with a shaved head, he was in his fifties and new to the city, he had just got transferred from Maldorn, a small town on the outskirts of the city, a nice place, very little crime. Officer Jacobs was assigned to the precinct, stark contrast to his previous gig

He responded in a deep tone with a slight accent. "Kids been sat here all morning, not budged once"

I turned to Hoffman facing my back to the officer, "Look at him!" I whispered looking at Adil through the glass. "He's a good kid, I can tell, why such horrific murders?"

Hoffman and I stood there staring at him through the glass for some time, we stood in silence, trying to read him, to see if he gave off any clues. I could feel Officer Jacobs getting uncomfortable.

Hoffman tapped my stomach, "C'mon, let's get this over with" We left the observation room and entered the interrogation room. We took our seats on the opposite side of the table. A real power move, straight out of the playbook, Hoffman ruffled some 'important' files together.

Adil was a young man, no older than twenty-one, with a short Afro cut hairstyle, he wore a dark blue t-shirt, grey sweatpants and sneakers. The black bracelet on his left wrist caught my eye, plaited cord wrapped five, maybe six times around his wrist, interloping straps of leather. It was the glint of the metal broach that gained my attention, Pavlov's electric dragonfly symbol, the same symbol found burned onto the victims bodies. He sat slouched in his seat, head down. Staring at the floor, paying no attention to his surroundings. He didn't care about the events to follow, he'd clearly given up.

I looked at him with curiosity and disgust. "The date is the seventh of August, I am Detective Costa, sat next to me, Detective Hoffman"

Hoffman cleared his throat, "We here interviewing Adil Abara for the murders of Captain Samira and two other unknown victims"

"Mira, not Samira" Adil whispered still looking at the floor

"Can you state your name for the record?" I wanted to keep things by the book, no way was he getting off on a technicality.

"Adil Abara. My name is Adil Abara"

Hoffman raised his eyebrows, "Why don't we start at the beginning, when did you first meet Captain Samira?"

Adil sat upright and leaned his elbows on the table "Seventeen years ago, She was my fathers captain...they were also dating"

"They were?" Hoffman asked

"Yes," Adil replied. "they kept it quiet from the police, didn't want it to interfere with work"

Adil started "Dad had just started as a cop, he didn't want it to be known he was dating a captain, that could have affected his career, it wasn't common for a captain to have.." Adil paused for a second, looking for the right word "...a relationship with rookie cop"

"An affair?" I suggested

"NO! They were both single, it was just something that happened between them, dad told me to keep quiet, not tell anyone"

"How long had this been going on?" Hoffman asked

"I dunno, a couple of years...I was young" Adil looked down again, it was surprising to see him so co-operative, after what he did, I expected a stuck up brat demanding attention.

"Did Captain Samira know about you?" Adil slammed his hands on the table in frustration. "What are you doing? I didn't kill Samira!"

Hoffman and I exchanged glances. "Just trying to clear the facts Mr Abara" I tried to calm him down.

Adil breathed deeply, anger fueled his body, this was his real side. The calm cooperative nature was a front, I could tell he had a troubled past.

"So, you say you didn't kill Captain Samira, Who did?" I asked, Adil ignored the question

"Mira was supposed to free them, same with Kara" Adil replied, his tone was sharp, cold and calculated. The way he spoke was not of the deaths of people, with lives and loved ones, but of simple objects, tools that failed to do the job.

"Free them?" I asked

Adil looked at me, "My father wasn't killed, but cursed" Adil explained through gritted teeth. "He's lost somewhere, in those orbs. The only way to save him is to torture and kill women who look like Samira, the one who loved him"

"What!" Hoffman shook his head in confusion, holding back laughter at the ridiculousness

"Those orbs, the one I dropped when you were chasing me," Adil explained. "They are cursed, they hold the lifeforce of victims." Adil Slammed his hands on the table "Victims taken by Pavlov and his Dragonflies!"

"I can't help but notice," I pointed at Adil's wrist. "You're wearing a dragonfly bracelet?" Adil covered up and slumped back down like a naughty child being caught by his mother. "Mr Abara, what's your involvement with Pavlov and the dragonflies?"

Hoffman was bewildered by all this, he took a deep breath and stood up from the table, and began to pace back and forth.

"Well?" I looked at him and waited for a response, using the awkward silence to my advantage. "Pavlov recruited kids, a few years back" Adil opened up "he used me, gained my trust. I was confused and young, angry at the world." tears began to fall down Adils face as he explained his childhood "When I learned about what he did, what he did to my father and how he could face me day to day, pretending to be my friend. I knew I had no chance against him, not in a one-on-one fight. I just needed to save my dad."

"We couldn't find any evidence that links these murders to Pavlov, are you telling us he killed your father and captain?" I needed it clear as day, in black and white. If we were going after Pavlov, I needed proof.

"That's how he took over the ACPD, turned it into the Arcane Abyss" Adil replied. "He's an evil man, he took my dad, he's trapped somewhere" Adil paused, he wiped away the sweat that had formed on his forehead. "Pavlov tricked my dad, he's in one of those orbs, I swear it!" Adil continued.

I rubbed my temples, all this was making my head hurt "So, Pavlov tricks Sgt. Abara 'Captures him', kills Captain Samira and takes over the ACPD" I listed the events back to Adil as I understood them "You on the other hand kill Mira and Kara, hoping that they'll release your father because Samira was killed the same way?" I asked

"Yes! I killed them, when I killed Kara in the old factory and nothing happened I knew" Adil slumped back into his chair "I knew I was wrong. Maybe dad's lost forever?" Adil's voice broke down, he started to cry, "I don't know" He whimpered.

I felt sorry for him, he had been through so much. Hoffman interjected "who were they to you?" Adil looked confused "Mira and Kara, did you know them?" Adil became agitated, like he hated this part and wanted to leave "I..um..dated Mira for sometime and.." Adil burst into tears, but this time i couldn't tell if it was for show or if it was genuine emotion "..I saw Kara working at the coffee shop on third, i was desperate, I drugged her on her lunch break, i kidnapped her and took her to the old factory, I swear.." Adil pleaded with us, trying to gain some sort of trust. By this time, it was enough. "I swear if I knew she had a kid, I wouldn't have." Adil sighed and muttered under his breath "he's all alone now, it's my fault" I had seen and heard enough, I knew what I had to do. "We're done Mr. Abara" I flagged Officer Jacobs, "take him away" I waved my hand towards the door

Adil stood from his chair and looked at me "Save him, there could be more. Pavlov has him. SAVE MY

FATHER!!" He begged as Jacobs escorted him out of the room, Officer Jacobs took him by the arm and led him towards the cells.

We left the interrogation room and walked towards the front door of the precinct, "We doing this? Are we really going after Pavlov?" Hoffman was nervous, I could tell he wasn't happy about what we had to do "It'll be a war, but we have reason to at least take him in for questioning" I tried to calm his nerve "In and out, no more than we have to"

We kept our cool, making sure not to gain attention from the other officers in the precinct, taking a sharp left into the armoury of the precinct, we knew each other well, we knew the plan, even if we didn't say a thing. I strapped a bulletproof vest over my body, I loaded my pistols and took extra clips, loading them one by one into my vest. I looked over at Hoffman who was also prepping, loading shells into a double barreled, pump action shotgun. Hoffman was a wrecking ball with that beast, exactly what we needed. "If he knows we're coming, it'll be tricky" Hoffman looked me in the eye "You know he'll be prepared for this, stay frosty!" He checked his weapon again "He has an arsenal at his disposal" Hoffman's voice was shaky and unsure, I knew how he felt, I felt it too.

I tilted my head towards the exit of the precinct, Hoffman led the way and we left out into the busy streets of Azurite City.

XII

The Old ways

It was around 9pm by the time we reached the Arcane Abyss, the usual rabble of punters gathered outside waiting to get in. "Fucking hell!" I exclaimed as Hoffman parked the car on the side of the street. "Hopefully, no one will remember us from a couple days ago"

At this time of the night the club was getting busy, there were two bouncers on the door. As we approached the club one of the bouncers called out "Evening Detectives, not here for a drink are you?" He had a confident smirk on him, someone tipped them off. Corruption ran deep in Azurite City, thugs on Pavlov's payroll were ex-cops, some were still on the beat. Anyone could have seen us at the station and gave Pavlov a heads up. It made my skin crawl, knowing I shared a precinct with bent coppers, too busy filling their pockets and not making the streets safe.

"Not quite," Hoffman replied, "Just looking for a bit of information. Hope you can help us."

"Oh yes?" the bouncer replied with a cheeky grin on his face.

"Need a chat with your boss" I slowly gripped my pistol

The bouncer looked Hoffman up and down as if he was considering letting us in.

"Nah. Sorry fellas" He pushed the door closed, he paused for a second with his back towards us before swinging a left hook at Hoffman's jaw, Hoffman quickly dodged to the side and kicked the bouncer's shin as hard as he could, causing the bouncer to topple forward, Hoffman then launched an uppercut sending the bouncer flying backward, knocking him unconscious. Hoffman moved aside as the second bouncer rushed in to attack, I threw a punch and caught the bouncer's fist before he had a chance to land a blow, I spun the attacker and flung him over my shoulder onto the concrete with a loud thud. I aimed my pistol at his forehead, "You got 5 seconds to fuck off"

The bouncer had a look of fear in his eyes, he got up and ran off into the city. Hoffman opened the door and we both walked into the club. As we descended the stairs, a group of girls blocked our path, one of them charged towards us with her sword raised, A long thin blade shaped for agility and precision. I stepped to the side as she came close and jabbed her in the ear. She quickly turned and attacked me again, I gripped her wrist and twisted the blade out of her hand. She pulled her side blade and slashed me across my right arm. I pulled back and punched her in the nose, as she fell back she knocked into some punters behind her. They didn't look too pleased but were reluctant to start anything, probably due to the fact we were cops. Nobody wanted to be seen helping cops. I took my chance and rushed her, throwing a punch. Frustratingly, she blocked with a spirit shield and kicked my stomach, sending me backwards. Steadying my balance, I launched another blow, this time she didn't block, catching her jaw, she flew into the wall. "Costa!" Hoffman shouted as I turned to see a second attacker forming a fireball, Hoffman fired his shotgun past my head, wisps of blues and greens flew as Hoffman muttered words of incantation "*Mahalarga-dreguula*" magic surrounded her as she burned, slowly turning to ash. I heard several screams as the crowd started to run away in terror, the music stopped and the club got eerily silent. The club had only a handful of staff left standing, some holding weapons. I saw Pavlov in his office watching the events unfold clapping sarcastically. "Bravo Fellas Bravo!" my attention snapped back to the group of employees advancing toward us, I swiftly pulled my pistols and opened fire. The shots missed their intended targets as they collided with the magical shield forming around them, blue sparks illuminated the room. "You gotta be kidding me!" Hoffman groaned. I lowered my pistol and looked around for another weapon. One of the punters ran up behind me, I guess he thought he could catch me off guard, his thumping footsteps gave him away. I twisted around and grabbed his ankle locking it tight, i began to twist causing him agonising pain, his head rolled back as he screamed "FUCK! Stop, please stop!" I kept twisting until his leg broke. I let go and pushed him forward onto the group of attackers, he tripped a couple of them up. "NOW!" Hoffman fired again, this time I felt the force of the impact as the bullets struck home. The shots tore through their bodies like butter, blood sprayed out as they fell to the floor. I jumped forward with my foot in the air, smashing down onto the neck of the fallen employee, a sickening crunch of his spine breaking followed. I glanced at Pavlov's office window, the door was shut. "Hoffman!" I shouted. He turned to see me running past the bodies towards the office door. "I'll hold them off" He loaded his shotgun and stood between me and the employees.

I looked for an obvious way in, nothing was apparent. The door had no keyhole or handle, the sound of Hoffman's shotgun blasting frantically had stopped "gawd damn! I've missed that" Hoffman slowly climbed the stairs looking proud covered in blood. "You ok?" I asked as he stood next to me, we were both out of breath.

I held my hands on the door, fingers stretched out wide "Khalli-dhall" the doors flung open, revealing the office. Pavlov stood proud with his dog beside him, he gently reached for a red vile inside his jacket pocket and violently grabbed his dog's head back, pouring the contents I could tell the dog knew what was about to happen, the defenceless whimpering turned into a deep, sopping growl. The beast was unleashed, Pavlov threw the vile at my feet. The beast charged ferociously, saliva flew in the air, I ran forward grabbing the beast by the jaws and clasped them shut. It shook, its eyes flashed bright blue, it growled and shook back and forth, I held it tightly as it scratched my hands. My fingers slipped and I fell back on the floor, the dog pounced on top of me, biting and scratching. Pavlov looked on with a grin on his face, he enjoyed the violence. I pushed the beast off me and stood up, I managed to muster up some energy, at this point I was panting just as hard as the dog. I charged at Pavlov, he raised his hand in the air, his index finger pointing towards me.

"No!" Hoffman shouted from behind me. My body lifted in the air, the force of his spell slammed me into the far wall, my back twisted, my body slumped as I hit the ground. The room began to spin, my vision blurred as I tried to focus on Pavlov who stood motionless. I struggled to my knees, everything hurt so much. "Fuck this" Hoffman shouted as he reached for his revolver and pointed it directly at the beasts head. "Hoffman, wait! "I pleaded with him, but my words were unheard, the loud boom rang through the room, the beast's blood splattering on my face, its limp body fell onto me, the red, viscous, sticky blood dripped onto my skin, The gargantuan beast shrivelled and shrunk back into the dog.

The warm trickle of blood ran down my neck, the metallic taste in my mouth made me nauseous. I tried to stand but the exhaustion was too great. Pushing the dog aside I reached for my pistol and stared down the barrel, locked in position. "Fuck you old man" I pulled the trigger. The bullets struck him in the chest, blood exploded out his chest and down his body. I kept firing, watching the body flail in pain. Pavlov collapsed on the floor, a pool of blood formed underneath him. Hoffman ran toward me "Costa! Are you alright?" I shook my head, struggling to focus on anything, I collapsed, I couldn't move, the pain was excruciating. The colour of my eyes changed from a warm brown to a cold sharp grey, my skin felt warm. I fell unconscious.

XIII

Evolution

Waking in a hospital bed, in a white room with no windows was a little jarring to say the least, thoughts rushed my mind. What happened at the Arcane Abyss? Was Hoffman ok? What is this place? I drifted in and out of consciousness. A soft familiar voice gently called my name, the figure of a woman stood by my bedside "Ant?...Antonio?" I turned my head, everything felt sore, "Liv?" I asked "Where?", she caressed my forehead "You don't remember? You've suffered great wounds, that beast tore you to shreds! It's been about 4 days. We were all so worried" She gently placed her hand on mine. I tried to move, it was so painful "shhh, relax. You're safe now" She placed her hand on my forehead. "Take it easy, I love you" I slowly moved my hand towards her face and softly moved her hair behind her ear. "I was so worried" She leaned in and kissed me, it was a passionate kiss, we embraced "I should get back to work, I'll come by tomorrow morning to check on you. Just rest and get well." I didn't want her to leave. This feeling was strange, Both Hoffman and I had been in hospital plenty of times, getting injured was all part of the job, but this was nothing like i'd ever felt before. She left the room, I drifted back to sleep.

Hoffman had nodded off a chair on the opposite side of my room. "Hey" I whispered. He slowly woke up, looking at me with a warm smile on his face. "Hey partner, how's your shoulder?" I replied with a slight smile "Fucking hurts, but I'll survive. How long was I out for?" I asked, still thinking about the case. Hoffman chuckled "About a week and a half, Liv's been helping out" I looked at Hoffman and thought for a minute, I could tell he knew something, but didn't want to say anything. "What, what is it?" Hoffman stood up and walked over to the bed. "Do you remember what happened, at the Arcane abyss?" Hoffman looked sorry for himself "err, yeah sure." I paused for a moment piecing the events "We fought a couple of thugs, entered Pavlov's office and killed him, dog too" Hoffman looked concerned "Not, quite Pavlov's dead, the dog's still alive" Liv walked into the room interrupting the conversation "Fantastic, your up!" she sat down next to Hoffman "It's good to see you awake" I nodded and looked at Hoffman who gave me a knowing look. "What's up Hoffman, spill it!" Hoffman looked over to Liv, "When i shot the beast and it fell on you, part of its DNA mixed with your own, " Hoffman walked over to the bedside table and picked up a mirror, "Look at your eyes" he held it in front of me, my eyes glowed sharply "Your vitals are fine, we need to run some tests when your on your feet, we have no idea why your eyes have changed or what else may have been affected" Liv stood on the other side of my bed and held my hand. "You'll be Ok" I could tell she was saying that for my benefit, and I pretended to be for hers.

The next few weeks flew by, stuck in a hospital bed didn't help, but the doc said I made a surprisingly speedy recovery. When I got out, it took a while for me to readjust to being active again, several rounds of physiotherapy assisted a full recovery. I was eager to get back to work, to finish the case. I made sure to check in with Liv at the precinct. walking through those front doors made me a little nervous, how would people take the new me? Heck! I didn't fully know what the new me was? I hoped Liv had answers.

As I climbed the steps that led to the bullpen, I was expecting officers to gather before the shift, finishing off their coffees and chatting about how their weekends went. It was suspiciously quiet, I could hear a few whispers in the background, excited voices shushing each other. "Congratulations!" floods of cheers filled the room and all eyes turned to me, joyous faces all happy to see me. Some of them reached out to shake my hand "Congratulations Detective! Pavlov's finally gone, well done!" My eyes scanned the room, where was she? Liv's smiling face caught my breath, I wanted to go over to her, the crowded room prevented me from showing my true affection, I smiled back.

"Uhh... thanks." I stuttered and looked around at all of the people watching me. Liv quickly darted through the crowd and hugged me tightly, she didn't care about the whispering gossipers.

"Everyone's really excited to have you back." she smiled up at me. "I kinda like the new eyes" I could feel her gaze roaming over my body as she said that. "They make you look kinda mysterious" her cheeky grin suggested something a little more.

I was a little unsure how to take all the attention, so I just smiled awkwardly and followed Liv downstairs to her lab. As soon as we were through the door she pushed me up against the wall. Her kisses were rough and demanding, as she pushed her tongue into my mouth and ground her hips against mine. My hands grabbed her by the ass and I hoisted her up, her legs wrapped around me, The kiss broke, and she pulled back just enough to look into my eyes. "Damn!" she sighed lustfully and kissed my neck. I carried her over to the desk, but she slid down from my grasp and pointed at the examination table. "Lie down" she ordered me. "I wanna get these tests to find out what that beast did to you" Liv was always business first "I feel stronger, quicker, like i'm on edge permanently." Liv had turned on her exam table. Holographic screens displayed multiple graphs and charts, I had no idea what they all meant. Mechanical arms locked me into place and scanned my entire body "Any clues doc?" As the scanning stopped I propped myself up with my elbows, watching her tap away on her computer, "It looks like the DNA of the beast mixed with your healing abilities, just a sec..." she continued to tap on the keyboard "Yes, just as I thought, please?" she held her hand out wanting me to stand near the far wall "what's going on, Doc?" Liv grabbed a gun from the rack on the wall "hold still!" she ordered. I raised my hands and looked at her questioningly "LIV?" she fired the gun, DEADSHOT! I stumbled back and looked at my chest, feeling for the wound. Nothing. I darted my eyes back at Liv, "Please tell me you knew that would happen!?" she smiled and shrugged her shoulders "Just a hunch" the bullet fell to the floor crumpled. "so...I'm bulletproof?" Liv raised her eyebrows "you've inherited the beast's perks and abilities whilst keeping your form and consciousness, must be from your healing capabilities...Fascinating!" She scribbled down some notes on the clipboard.

"Does this mean I can go back to work? I've got a lot of paperwork."

Liv didn't answer, she was too busy scribbling down her notes. "Doc? Does this mean I can go back to work?"

"Hmm? Oh yes, of course, it's up to you. your vitals are more than great, so i don't see why not" she smiled at me "I'm glad your back"

"Thanks Liv." I said as I turned to leave. "Hey! What do you want for dinner? my treat" she called out after me.

"You pick"

XIV

Reunion

As I walked back up to the bullpen, the animal handler approached me with Pavlov's dog, the dog had blood all over him and was very weak. "Where are you going with him?" I looked down at him, whimpering and shivering "Doctor Harlow wants to run tests then get him over to the rescue centre" Animal handlers were rare to come by, Only a few in the city. He didn't know his way around. "Second door on the left"

By this time Hoffman had arrived and was at his desk, finishing up some paperwork, going over last checks. "Ay, it's good to see you back!" Hoffman stood up, too excited to see me, flinging his chair backward "back in action!" We hugged like two brothers seeing each other after a long spring break.

"How's the case coming along?" I was eager to get back to work, I didn't like leaving things unfinished. "Just gotta escort Adil to prison and send Pavlov's dog to the pound, other than that case is closed bud, I waited for you" He placed his hand on my shoulder and smiled "they're waiting now", We turned toward the cells when the animal handler from before ran up to me "Detectives" He was panting, out of breath, struggling to squeeze out his sentences "Detectives....Doc....Help!" I looked at Hoffman in horror, we ran down the stairs and burst through the door. "Liv!" I shouted in desperation "LIV!" her office was built in an 'L' shape formation and her examination table was just out of sight "Detectives! I'm fine, please come take a look!" she waved us over in excitement, as she walked over to her desk she reached for a syringe, "I've run some tests, Detective Costa" She was always professional no matter the circumstance, "Detective Costa, you were attacked by this dog?" I looked at her clueless to where she was going with this "Err, yeah. Not like this, he was huge when he attacked" Liv smiled back at me, she had pieced it all together That is because.." She filled the syringe with blue swirling, pearlescent liquid. slowly she pushed the needle into the dogs neck and squeezed the plunger "You might want to stand back!" she held her arm out pushing me back. The dog began to shake, convulse, and foam at the mouth, he fell to the ground writhing in pain. "What did you do?!" I ran over to the dog trying to hold him still, Hoffman joined in and helped pin down his legs. "I just injected antitoxin! The poison was injected into the bloodstream turning him into this, the antitoxin will neutralise the effects! That's why he's been attacking people, it's the same poison Nyx had but in a much smaller dose, she couldn't handle it however because she was already a panther, adding to her animalistic nature was too much for her to handle."

The dog shed its fur, bald. He grew in size slowly morphing into a man, a great hulking goliath "Sgt. Abara?" Hoffman couldn't believe his eyes. Abara raised his hands, moving the digits one by one, he began to stroke his arms and moved slowly to his face "No, No, this can't be" relief overwhelmed the Sergeant as he fell to his knees. Hoffman ran out the room "One sec, I'll be back!" "I've killed so many! He made me kill so many!" Abara wept into his hands as we all stood there in silence, in shock. Hoffman returned out of breath and grinning. I hadn't a clue what he was up to. Hoffman grabbed the sheet covering the lab bed and wrapped it around the Sergeants naked waist. "Dad?" Adil came running into the room, confused and in shock he stood in the middle of the room, his eyes filled with tears "Dad?" Adil leaped into his fathers arms "So, many years" Adil cried "So many years, i've searched" He wiped his tears away and looked up at his father, who's expression was solemn. "I'm sorry son" Abara spoke in a quiet tone "Pavlov tricked me, he..." Adil pulled away and stared his father in the eyes "I've done things dad, awful things. I'm scared" I looked at Hoffman then tilted my head towards the door "Listen," Hoffman cleared his throat "We'll give you some time" we left the Sgt and his son in the room alone as we stood guard on the other side, we waited for about an hour before we heard a knock on the door "It's time" Sgt Abara opened the door, I walked over to Adil, he looked like a scared little boy "I'm ready" he took a deep breath and straightened his back, "Thank you" looking and Hoffman and I "Thank You detectives, I know he's alive. I must pay for what i've done" We escorted Adil to the precinct garage, the van was parked waiting. Adil climbed into the van as he looked back at us, he looked calm, at peace.

Sgt Abara, over time, regained his position in the Police force. With Pavlov gone the Sgt took back control of the ACPD precinct in downtown and with that the Arcane Abyss was no longer. Detectives Costa and Hoffman continued their good work alongside Sergeant Abara. With Costa's new abilities he became a vital asset to the team. Adil served three years in prison, he spent his time alone and didn't associate himself with any of the gangs inside, unfortunately during a riot between two rival gangs, Adil was in the wrong place at the wrong time, stabbed seventeen times Adil was killed. Doctor Harlow and Detective Costa's relationship grew stronger and the Doc moved in with Costa.

Printed in Great Britain
by Amazon

44818109R10067